The Catch Colt

OTHER SAGEBRUSH LARGE PRINT WESTERNS BY
LAURAN PAINE

Bags and Saddles

Buckskin Buccaneer

Guns of the Law

Six-Gun Atonement

The Californios

The Past Won't End

The Rawhiders

Valor in the Land

The Catch Colt

LAURAN PAINE

Sagebrush
Large Print Westerns

Library of Congress Cataloging in Publication Data

Paine, Lauran.
   The catch colt / Lauran Paine.
      p.   cm.
ISBN 1-57490-249-0 (alk.paper)
1.Large type books. I. Title.

PS3566.A34 C38 2000   99-054896
813'.54—dc21

Cataloguing in Publication Data is available from The British Library
and the National Library of Australia.

Sagebrush Large Print Westerns are published in the United
States and Canada by Thomas T. Beeler, Publisher, Box 659,
Hampton Falls, New Hampshire 03844-0659. ISBN 1-57490-249-0

Published in the United Kingdom, Eire, and the Republic of South
Africa by Isis Publishing Ltd, 7 Centremead, Osney Mead, Oxford
OX2 0ES England. ISBN 0-7531-6247-4

Published in Australia and New Zealand by Bolinda Publishing
Pty Ltd, 17 Mohr Street, Tullamarine, Victoria, 3043, Australia.
ISBN 1-86442-019-X

Manufactured by Sheridan Books in Chelsea, Michigan

The Catch Colt

CHAPTER 1

Approaching Autumn

WHEN LANKY, TURKEY-NECKED HUGH PEPPERDINE was firing up the wood stove under his coffeepot the sun was breaking clear of some autumn-hazed distant rims. The town was beginning to stir around him, and that damn fool who'd recently acquired the smithy at the southern end of Sheridan was making enough noise to raise the dead as he warped steel across an anvil.

Hugh had been the local saddle- and harnessmaker in Sheridan for about as many years as some of the other merchants were old. Like James McGregor, the gunsmith whose shop was catty-corner from the leather works on the east side of Main Street, Hugh's outlook, which had been formed by a frontier existence that had rarely been mild, was a country mile from being noticeably altruistic or excessively tolerant.

When the kindling was popping he shoved in a scantling of dry oak, slammed the stove's door, and went around behind the counter to his work area. He plucked a stained old apron off the wall where tin templates hung, and while tying it into place heard spurred bootfalls crossing over out front and turned.

His first customer of the day was old Davy Barber, who ran cattle in the Sheridan Plain area during the warm months and trailed everything south into northern Arizona before a northern winter set in.

He was a raffish man of indeterminate years with a predatory expression, testy gray eyes, and, rumor had it, more money than Carter had pills. It was typical of them

1

both that neither smiled as they exchanged a "good morning."

Davy shoved back his disreputable old sweatstained hat, wrinkled his nose in the direction of the coffeepot, and said, "You don't sleep in either, eh? A man once told me folks that don't sleep in got bad consciences. You believe that, Hugh?"

Pepperdine finished tying the apron, regarded the shorter, equally as gray and grizzled man, and jutted his jaw Indian-fashion in the direction of the stove. "It's hot if you want a cup." As the cowman turned he also said, "Unless you bedded down in town last night, Mr. Barber, then you had to get up a hell of a long time before I did to ride into Sheridan this morning, so maybe that feller was right."

Davy Barber accepted this insulting innuendo with his back to the harnessmaker as he filled a cup with coffee as black and malevolent as original sin. Then he turned, leaned on the counter with the cup, and eyed the taller man. "I rode in to look up Marshal Fogarty."

Pepperdine was unrolling some damp croaker sacks that had a seating leather inside them when he replied. "Try the cafe. I usually see him walk past across the road but this morning I wasn't watching. If he's not there try the jailhouse."

Davy Barber tasted the coffee, which had the aroma of diluted skunk scent and the taste of air-slacked lime. He put the cup aside for only one reason: it was too hot. For a long moment he watched Hugh place a pattern over the seating leather, check it on all sides, then hang it back on its nail. "New saddle, eh?" he said.

Hugh grunted. "Yeah. For a neighbor of yours."

"Buster Henning?"

"Yeah."

2

"That seatin' leather better fit a sixteen-inch saddle. Since he come back from Denver he don't look the same. Must have put on twenty pounds down there."

Hugh looked around at the saddle tree held firmly in place atop a sewing horse. "I know. He was in here couple of weeks ago." Hugh placed the damp cutout on the tree above the skived underlayer. Davy watched, tried the coffee again, found it no hotter than he was accustomed to, and leaned there watching and sipping.

Hugh, who had long accepted the fact that people sometimes hung out in his shop for hours, mostly when Rusty Morton's saloon wasn't open, went about his work, ignoring the cowman's presence until Davy said, "We're fixin' to go south."

Hugh nodded about that. It was autumn. "A little earlier'n last year, Mr. Barber."

"Yes, well, the smell of winter's a mite stronger this year."

Five minutes of silence ensued during which Hugh, satisfied the seating leather would fit, put it aside and worked on the fork covering. Davy watched this, too, sipped his coffee, and when Town Marshal Fogarty strode southward across the road, he saw him and continued to lean there.

Hugh finally stopped to look up. "Joe just went past. You see him?"

Barber nodded, sipped the last of the coffee, and pushed the cup aside as he said, "Hugh, you need a helper in here."

Pepperdine's eyes widened a little. "Do I? You come in here maybe two, three times a year, but you know I need a helper?"

Barber was fishing for a plug in his shirt pocket when he replied. "If you had an apprentice, it'd take you

3

maybe six, eight months to teach him enough for him to be worth a damn."

Hugh straightened up to his full height on the far side of the cutting table and watched the cowman tuck a cud into his cheek.

Davy's predatory expression now looked slightly lopsided. He was a lifelong chewer; he did not expectorate. Amateur tobacco chewers did that. "I got a young buck working for me who's exactly what you need in here, Hugh," he said while looking hard at the saddle tree atop the sewing horse. "Young, learns quick, works hard, strong and . . . Tell you what, Hugh: You set an apprentice's wages, an' I'll pay them for eight months." Barber's testy gaze came up. He was waiting.

Pepperdine shook his head; it was too early in the morning for this sort of thing. Barber misinterpreted the headwag. "I'm makin' you one hell of a proposition," he said, and didn't allow the saddlemaker to interrupt. "He's smart as a whip. He's been ridin' for me all season. He can rope with the best of them, shoe, do chores at the markin' grounds. The other riders like him."

Hugh went over to the wood stove, filled a cup from the pot, and returned to the working area with it. He put the cup down and looked steadily at the other older man for a moment before speaking. "Tell me somethin' Mr. Barber. If he's that good why don't you just keep him on and let him trail south with you?"

"He don't want to go."

"I see. Well then, just pay him off, an' if he hangs around up here, an' he's such a good hand and all, he could maybe get hired on dunging out at the liverybarn or maybe over at the smithy."

Barber's slatey gaze drifted from the saddle tree to

4

the patterns on the back wall, to the ceiling, and back down to Pepperdine. "He needs a trade, Hugh." "Cow boyin' is a trade."

"I just told you; he don't want to leave this area. There's no ridin' jobs in wintertime in the Sheridan country. . . .Tell you what, Hugh; I got a lot of harness needs overhauling. If you was to drive out this evenin' about suppertime you could look the lad over. On the sly, you understand. Sort of think it over and at the same time pick up all that harness to haul back and repair for me. An' have a decent supper."

Hugh stood like stone staring at the shorter, equally as old, tough cowman. When he did not respond, Davy Barber shoved up off the counter, reset his hat, said, "See you out there," and walked out of the shop.

Pepperdine drank some coffee, took the cup with him to the front window, and watched Barber cross over and head in the direction of the cafe.

Catty-corner northward James McGregor was sweeping the duckboards in front of the gun shop. Hugh put his cup aside and walked over there. The sun was above the rims now, and while it had no warmth yet, its brilliance burned the shadows away even on the east side of Main Street where McGregor leaned on his broom watching his old friend cross toward him.

McGregor was close to average height, but because he was big-boned and a ruggedly put-together individual he looked shorter. He was a widower. He was also a silversmith because gunsmithing, even in a country where everyone owned at least one gun, provided little more than a bare-bones livelihood.

As Pepperdine called a greeting, McGregor leaned the broom aside, scratched his reddish thatch, and returned the greeting. He turned to lead the way back

5

inside where the predominant odor was of oil and pipe smoke.

When Hugh began speaking the gunsmith leaned on his scarred counter listening, his eyes fixed on the taller man.

When Hugh finished McGregor shoved upright. "Care for some coffee?" he asked.

Pepperdine declined, shifted his cud to the other cheek, and watched his old friend get a cupful for himself. McGregor was a taciturn man, more so with some folks than with others. With Hugh Pepperdine, because they'd been through a lot together, he was blunt. "Well, what do you expect he's up to? I mean, besides tryin' to find a place for this rider of his."

Hugh had no idea, but he did have suspicions. "You know Davy as well as I do. He's as tight as the bark on a tree. When he offers to pay someone's wages for eight months, he's not doin' it from the goodness of his heart. If he's got a heart."

"Did you agree to go out there tonight?"

Hugh hadn't, but that load of harness that needed mending was a strong inducement. "Not exactly."

McGregor's pate eyes sparked. "What does 'not exactly' mean?"

"I can use the business, James."

McGregor's flinty features relaxed into a shrewd, faint smile. "An' he knows it. That was his bait, eh?"

"I expect so. You want to ride out in the wagon with me tonight?"

McGregor did not say he would or he wouldn't. He said, "Do you need an apprentice?"

"Like I need a truss. But if it don't cost me a dime for eight months . . ."

McGregor nodded to himself about something he was

6

turning over in his mind. "No thanks. You go get the load of busted harness, and I'll see you tomorrow. Besides, Joe Fogarty cracked the stock on his Winchester, and he wants it fixed by tomorrow. It'll take me most of the afternoon just to whittle a new stock to fit." He gazed dispassionately at the harnessmaker for a moment before saying more. "Hugh, think on it. That old bastard never gave anything away in his life, an' he's too old to start now. He's up to somethin' as sure as we're standing here. You be damned careful what you commit yourself to out there."

Pepperdine started to speak when McGregor gestured. "Someone just walked in over yonder."

Hugh glanced over his shoulder in the direction of his place of business, said a hasty, "See you tomorrow", and hurried back the way he'd come.

CHAPTER 2

An Argument

THE SADDLEMAKER'S SECOND CUSTOMER OF THE DAY was Town Marshal Fogarty, and he didn't put a dime in Pepperdine's cash drawer either, but he had a cup of coffee and explained why he'd come by.

"At breakfast this morning Silas Browning told me one of his stages came in last night with two torn tugs. He said he was too busy to come down here so would I ask you to go up there and get them?"

Hugh, who had about as much use for the stage company's local corralyard boss as other people around town, sighed loudly. Big Joe Fogarty, who was roughly half Pepperdine's age, laughed. "Yeah, I know; he could

7

send those tugs down with one of his yardmen. Well, I told you, which is all I said I'd do. By the way, wasn't that Davy Barber I saw leave here about the time you opened up?"

"Yes. I told him you'd be down at the cafe. You didn't meet him?"

"No. I was over at the jailhouse when I saw him enter the cafe."

"He didn't cross the road? I told him if you wasn't havin' breakfast you'd be at your office."

"Never came near. What'd he want? It was pretty early for someone to be in town who had to ride six or eight miles to get here."

Hugh balanced the explanation in his mind then decided against revealing it for no reason he understood himself. "Maybe rode in for the mail. Maybe to see who he could find to weasel out of some money. All right, I'll go up there for the harness tugs."

After Joe Fogarty departed Hugh went to work on the new saddle, but his mind was elsewhere. He and Davy Barber were acquaintances, not friends. He'd done a little work for the cowman over the years and had had to grit his teeth each time because Barber had to have an itemized bill for everything, including the thread used and the amount of harnessmaker's beeswax Hugh had used on the thread.

Hugh Pepperdine, who wore an oversized hat, Davy Barber and that wizened, old coot at the corral yard loathed people who either used tobacco or drank whiskey because, as hardshell Baptists, they knew these were the Devil's instruments, pried out of the same mold.

About noon he tossed the apron aside and went up to the corralyard. Silas Browning was not there but his yard boss was, a portly Mexican with a badly pockmarked face. They found the damaged harness, and while Hugh was examining it the Mexican said, "The horses shied and tore things."

Hugh looked up. Horses had to shy like hell to tear double-stitched, doubled leather harness tugs. The Mexican understood the look and shrugged. "It was gettin' dark, the driver said. He was comin' south out of the foot hills ready to make the straight run to town. About where he was leveling out something crouching back off the road on the west side suddenly rose up, all whitelike. The horses damn near turned the stage over." The Mexican grinned. "*Fantasma, amigo.*"

Hugh was gathering up the harness to fling it over a shoulder when he dryly said, "Sure. Is that what the driver said—a ghost? More'n likely a bear."

"No. He didn't know what it was. He was too busy tryin' to keep the hitch from bolting to even look back." The Mexican walked with Hugh as far as the pole gates. When they halted he looked straight at Pepperdine. "You ever see a white bear?"

Hugh shook his head. "I never saw a ghost either. Tell Silas it'll be a day or two."

The Mexican remained in place for a long moment, watching Hugh walk southward, then shrugged again and turned back into the yard.

Although the leaves were turning around town and elsewhere, the result of two recent black frosts, the days remained warm. Hazy-warm and windless. By midafternoon it was difficult to make out the northward mountains. Hugh had dumped the harness on the floor and was back working on the new saddle when a sturdy old wide-tired springless wagon pulled up out front and Davy Barber climbed down, leaving a lithe youth to

9

mind the horses.

Hugh went out when Barber called and beckoned as he freed some chain and dropped the tailgate. Hugh stood gazing at the tangle of harness for a moment then wordlessly joined Barber and the lithe, younger man lugging it all inside to be dumped in a pile in a corner.

It was a shame how people treated leather goods, like leaving them in the rain and wiring them in places when they broke or greasing everything else in a cow cap except harness leather then complaining about poor quality when the leather cracked and curled.

The cowboy returned to the wagon, climbed onto the seat, and sat there looking around as though he hadn't been in a whole lot of towns. Davy Barber said, "Saved you a trip out yonder tonight, Hugh. When I got back the cook was off his feed, and the riders were unhappy about not bein' able to find some of the bulls, so what the hell, me'n the lad loaded the wagon and brought this stuff in." Barber was gazing at the mound of harness as he spoke. "Enough to keep you busy for a couple of weeks, wouldn't you say?"

Hugh was also regarding the harness. "Maybe that long."

"Well, you got a new saddle to finish, and there's another set of harness over yonder; work's pilin' up on you, partner."

Barber was grinning, little shrewd eyes fixed on the harnessmaker. Hugh turned slowly to look out where the cowboy was lounging on the wagon seat. "That's him, Mr. Barber?"

"Yep. An' you don't have to 'mister' me. We been friends a long while. I'm just plain Davy."

Hugh turned back. Barber had been to town twice the same day, which was one hell of a ride or drive for no better reason than to dump some old harness on someone's floor. He said, "You'll be heading south when—next month?"

"About then. But don't worry about havin' the harness fixed before we pull out. I got other harnesses."

"But you'd like to have it before you leave?"

Barber spread both hands. "Sure. But if you can't because—"

"Mr. Barber, explain somethin' to me. You're almighty anxious for me—someone anyway—to take that lad over. Why? An' don't give me a lot of crap about him bein' such a good man and all, someone who needs to learn a trade."

The cowman's easy smile faded gradually as he and Pepperdine stood looking steadily at each other. Barber slowly reached into a pocket, drew forth a soft doeskin pouch, and placed it on the counter. "Eight months wages at the goin' rate for a rider. I've been told that's maybe a little more'n apprentices make in harness shops."

Hugh ignored the pouch. "You goin' to give me an answer or not?"

"You don't need no answer, you just need to pocket that money and teach the lad a trade. An' fix that harness when you'n him get around to it."

Hugh turned, eyed the sprawling youth again, turned back, hefted the little pouch under Davy Barber's calculating gaze, and said, "Keep it. An' take that harness somewhere else, maybe down to Bordenton to have it patched." He roughly pushed the pouch into the shorter man's hand and stalked around to his worktable to retrieve his apron and tie it into place.

Barber was motionless, holding the pouch of money as he watched Pepperdine start working on the saddle.

11

Somewhere down near the middle of town a dogfight erupted, and until it had been broken up Davy Barber neither moved nor spoke; but when the tumult ended he leaned on the counter, looking annoyed.

"Is there somethin' wrong with a man wantin' to see a decent young buck get started out right in life?"

Hugh replied without straightening back from his work. "No. Unless it's you."

Barber reddened. "Say that again!"

Hugh finally turned away from his work to face the cowman. "Mr. Barber, I only know you well enough from doin' work for you to know that you don't part with a red cent nor give anyone the benefit of a doubt unless it ends up in your favor." Hugh paused to glance toward the roadway briefly, then continued. "Now maybe that's the way life is; maybe that's why you got a lot of cattle and plenty of money, and all I got is this shop."

"Hugh, all I'm tryin' to do is see that the lad gets a better start than you'n I had."

Hugh nodded over that, then said, "Why?"

Barber was a long time replying. "You want me to write it out on a paper for crissake? I been tellin' you; he's bright an' decent and deserves better'n he's had so far. Listen to me: take the money, keep him around until I get back next spring—"

"What's wrong with him learnin' the cattle business? You've done well at it, so have a lot of other folks. It's a good trade with a good future."

Davy Barber shifted his stance, gazed at Hugh, and gently wagged his head. "First off, he don't want to be a cowman. He wants to stay in one place, maybe someday own a business in town. Hell, I can't blame him for that. You know how long's it taken me to get where I am? A whole damned lifetime, startin' out huntin' down wild cattle skinny as a snake to peddle for six bits a head." Barber paused. "I'm willin' to pay you for him and give you my business." Barber looked almost desperate. "Just for crissake give him a chance."

Hugh studied the cowman for a long time before turning back to his worktable. Moments passed; Barber watched everything Pepperdine did without once looking away, and when Hugh finally put the tools down and walked over to the counter the cowman had sweat on his face even though it wasn't that warm in the shop.

Hugh said, "How old is he?"

"Eighteen this past June."

"Where's he from; who're his folks?"

Barber replied to the last question first, very quickly. "He's an orphan. He comes from around San Luis. You know the place, about forty, fifty miles north through the mountains."

Hugh did indeed know the town of San Luis. He'd been up there many times. He turned slowly to look out the window again. The youth was no longer lounging on the wagon seat; he was carrying buckets of water from a trough across the road to the team horses.

He was tall for eighteen and didn't have a spare ounce of meat on him anywhere. Hugh sighed and turned back. He'd never had children, had in fact never been married. But that wasn't a child out there. If he had been once, whatever he might have retained from his childhood ways would have been roughed out of him after working for someone like Davy Barber. Hugh had another couple of questions. "Can he write 'n do sums?"

Barber hesitated over that. "Well, sort of. But, hell, I can't do them things very good either. Dammit, Hugh,

13

all you got to do is learn him a trade. The rest of it he'll have to pick up himself as he goes along."

Barber seemed to sense that Pepperdine's earlier resolve was weakening, because he sweetened the pot a little. "I need a new saddle. No neck nor belly leather, just from the back. I'll pick it up on my way through next spring, but I'll pay you for it right now. How much?"

Hugh considered his scarred, big hands before replying. He almost wanted to laugh. To his knowledge no one had ever bested Davy Barber. He wished James McGregor and Marshal Fogarty could hear this.

"New saddle, no skimping, forty dollars, an' like you said, next spring. You'll get your harness then, too."

Barber plunged a hand into a trouser pocket, counted out the crumpled bills like he was giving blood, and straightened up off the counter. His eyes were sparkling. "Keep your end of the bargain, Hugh."

Pepperdine smiled. "I always do, but if it comes out there's somethin' wrong . . ." He continued to smile as he pressed the greenbacks under big hands and said, "He's got his bedroll and all with him?"

"Yes."

"Go tell him to bring 'em in."

Barber let go a rattling sigh and walked out into the sunshine.

Hugh remained where he was, in the shop behind the counter, so he could not see James McGregor over in front of the gun shop watching as Davy Barber and the lanky youth unloaded a bag, a bedroll, an old saddle, and two guns, one long, one short, from beneath the seat of the wagon.

McGregor watched the cowboy and Barber disappear into the harness works and went back behind his own

14

counter to resume whittling on a maple gun stock.

He'd have bet his life Hugh got skinned by Davy Barber. He thought Hugh probably deserved it, too, after being warned about the cowman.

Joe Fogarty's big frame filled the doorway, and McGregor looked up. "Workin' on it," he told the town marshal.

Fogarty watched for a while, got a cud pouched into his cheek, and said, "What's goin' on over at the harness shop?"

McGregor replied without looking up from his work on the maple gun stock. "I'm not sure except that Barber wanted Hugh to hire some kid that's been ridin' for him as an apprentice. An' it looks like Hugh agreed. I just saw 'em carryin' somebody's gatherings into the shop."

Fogarty sat in an old wired-together chair before speaking again. "I know that kid. His name's Jefferson. I think his first name is George. He comes from the backcountry up around San Luis."

McGregor stopped working. "You know any reason why Davy Barber would pay good money for Hugh to teach him the harnessmaker's trade?"

"No. About all I remember about him was that a year or two ago the constable up there disarmed him in the middle of the roadway for challengin' some card dealer. He wasn't any more'n maybe about fifteen at the time. The constable pointed him out to me. He was working for a horse trader back then. The reason I remembered him was because only a damned fool kid would call a grown man an' a card dealer at that."

McGregor filled a foul little pipe and fired it up. "I don't know about the lad, Marshal, but I do know about Davy Barber, an' I warned Hugh to be awful damned

15

careful. Barber don't have a reputation for helpin' folks out."

Joe Fogarty arose, eyed the gun stock, and said, "I'll go over there. Will that thing be ready tomorrow?"

"Yes. Tomorrow afternoon. You never did say how you cracked the original stock."

"Tryin' to prize a big rock off what looked like a grave up near the northward foothills, and before you say it I know Winchesters aren't crowbars."

McGregor puffed and did not even look up until after the big town marshal had departed. Then he removed the pipe, spat unerringly into a brass spittoon, and shook his head. With all the tree limbs and whatnot in those foothills a man who'd use a perfectly good carbine for prying didn't have the sense the Good Lord had given a goose.

McGregor finally quit because it was getting darker inside his shop than it was out in the roadway. It was suppertime anyway or close to it. It was this time of day the pain of losing his wife hit him the hardest. Not just because he'd been eating out of cans or cowtown cafes since her passing, but because autumn evenings they'd strolled the acidy-scented countryside hand-in-hand, planning the family they'd never had, the business they'd make prosper with both of them working at it, and the years to come, which had indeed come, with McGregor alone with a heartache that even after twenty-five years had lessened very slightly if at all.

CHAPTER 3

The Apprentice

JOE FOGARTY HAD COME AND GONE, AND THE LANKY youth had stowed his belongings in a lean-to back room and listened expressionlessly to everything Hugh told him. He was mute as a stone, which made it both awkward and exasperating for Hugh, who had never before tried to teach anyone what he knew of the saddle-and-harness trade. His best efforts and his patience did not draw the lad out of himself.

In fact, the boy scarcely spoke at all for several days, but he learned rapidly, as that old devil Barber had said he could, and he had a gift. When Hugh'd first started out he couldn't sew a straight line to save his soul. George Jefferson didn't do too well on his first harness tug, but on the second one, when Hugh examined it by window-light, the seam was perfectly straight with even tension on all the stitches.

McGregor ambled over on the fourth day to drink coffee and discuss the weather while gazing candidly over where the youth was finishing those traces Silas Browning's yardboss had given to Pepperdine.

Hugh dug McGregor in the ribs, called to the youth he'd be back directly, and took the gunsmith out front and across to Rusty Morton's Drover's Rest Saloon. They took a bottle with two jolt glasses to a far table, and the moment Pepperdine was seated he said, "What the hell do you have to stare for? He's feelin' lost enough as it is."

McGregor sipped his whiskey. "Does he have any

promise?"

"Yes. He can sew straight and cut patterns an' he's only been here three days. This is his fourth day."

"Don't talk much, does he?"

"Neither would you or me if we was dumped in a strange town among folks we didn't know."

James considered his empty jolt glass. "What'd Joe have to say when he come by a few days back?"

"Say? I introduced him, they shook hands, George went back to work, and the marshal had a cup of coffee with me talkin' about all the signs pointin' to an early snow this year."

"He didn't tell you he knew the lad, or that he called a loan shark up in San Luis?"

Hugh sat back. Marshal Fogarty hadn't mentioned knowing who George was. "He told you that?"

"Yep, An' that the lad was raised in the backcountry up there."

Hugh emptied his glass to gain a little time. "Called a loan shark? You mean with a gun?"

"Yep. In the middle of Main Street up there. About two years ago."

Pepperdine did some arithmetic in his head. "He's only eighteen now. That'd have been when he was about fifteen."

"So the marshal said."

They refilled the little glasses, and Hugh's demeanor changed. He'd been annoyed before; now he was beginning to worry.

McGregor watched his friend's face and made a bleak little smile. "I warned you not to have dealings with Davy Barber."

Round-faced, pale-skinned Rusty Morton called from behind his bar. "James, the mail just come in."

The pair of older men returned to the roadway where McGregor walked briskly on a diagonal course across the road toward the corralyard. He'd been expecting a box of new lightning Colt pistols, and they were a month overdue.

Hugh ambled back to the shop where George was plucking threads from a cracked, badly neglected saddle skirt and only glanced up to nod. Hugh got a cup of coffee at the stove and stood holding it, watching the youth work. Several blue-tailed flies were hitting the front window to make the only noise until a battered old ranch wagon rattled past in the direction of Hank Dennis's general store.

George finally put the skirt down, wiped his hands on his old britches, and said, "There's the feller's name who brought this skirt in while you was over at the saloon."

Hugh went to the counter to study the scrap of paper. He knew the cowman who'd been in during his absence. Below the name was one word: "Tomorrow."

Hugh set the cup aside. "You told him it'd be ready tomorrow?"

"Yes."

"There's other work ahead of it, George."

"I'll finish it tonight after supper."

Hugh picked up the cup, eyed the skirt, and shook his head. "You're goin' to learn something on that job," he told the youth. "First off, when you get all the thread out, you got to clean the leather real good. Damned cowmen never, ever bring anything in here that's not just about beyond doin' anything with. Then you got to lightly oil it, from the underside, always from the underside. Then you got to cut the pelt, sponge it and stretch it, sew it and trim it. George, next time tell 'em

19

it'll be maybe a week."

Without raising his head the lad said, "I told you—I'll work on it tonight. He wanted it tomorrow. I told him he could have it by then."

Hugh straightened back off the counter, sipped coffee that was now lukewarm, and said nothing until he was ready to go back fitting leather over the new saddle. Then all he said was, "Next time tell 'em a week."

The blue-tailed flies were still striking glass and continued to do so; otherwise the silence in the shop was thick enough to cut with a knife, and the longer Hugh worked the more fiercely annoyed he became with Davy Barber.

But he was an honest man; all the blame did not lie with the cowman.

Shortly before lock-up time he went up to the bank and deposited the money Barber had given him. Then he returned to the shop, lighted three coal-oil lamps so George could see what he was doing, still without a word passing between them, hung up his apron, and headed for supper over at the cafe.

The town doctor was over there. His pretty wife had gone down to Bordenton to fetch back some supplies for her husband, otherwise wild horses couldn't have dragged Henry Pohl to the cafe for supper.

When Hugh eased down at the counter the doctor looked around, nodded, and went back to his meat for a moment before turning more slowly to study Pepperdine's face. He said, "We all have bad days, Hugh," to which the harnessmaker made a grumbling retort.

"But not for eight months, Henry."

Doctor Pohl put down his knife and fork. "You have an ailment?"

20

"No, I have a kid Davy Barber palmed off on me for an apprentice."

"So I heard. Something wrong with him?"

"I can't put my finger on it, Henry. He don't talk, but, hell, lots of folks don't talk."

"He's not working out?"

"Working out? He's already picked up more'n I did at his age."

"Then what is it?"

Hugh shook his head, called his order to the cafeman, and changed the subject. "I told you, I can't put my finger on it. Anyway, how's the doctorin' business?"

Doctor Pohl went back to his meal as he replied. "Brisk. Delivered three babies this week, set a broken arm, dosed the blacksmith's helper with calomel for whatever ails him, which I privately think is secret drinking, and lanced a boil as big as your palm on a ring-tailed bull for a stockman east of town."

Marshal Fogarty walked in, acknowledged several greetings, and sat down on the opposite side of Pepperdine. He called his order then leaned back with clasped hands, looking around. When his attention settled on Hugh he said, "How's George making it?"

Hugh had to lean back for the cafeman to put a platter in front of him as he replied. "He's a good worker, learns fast . . . Why didn't you tell me he got into a fight with a gambler up at San Luis?"

"How could I with him standing right there? Anyway, what's that got to do with how he's working out with you?"

Hugh didn't know what it had to do with it. "He don't say ten words all day. It's hard to figure a man who don't talk."

Fogarty gave Hugh a rough slap on the shoulder as

·21

his own meal arrived and went to work feeding a very large, powerful frame. Fortunately Marshal Joe Fogarty was neither accustomed to woman-cooked meals nor very particular about what he ate.

When Hugh went outside to use his wicked-bladed clasp knife to whittle off a cud of molasses-cured Kentucky twist, night was settling. Rusty Morton's business was picking up at the saloon, judging from the number of horses tethered to his rack in front of the saloon, and directly opposite lights blazed in the harness shop. That damned kid was going to be up half the night, maybe longer, working on that old saddle skirt.

Hugh spat into the dusty roadway and ambled down toward the lower end of town where the smithy was almost directly opposite the public corrals and the combination livery-trading barn. He hadn't owned a horse in fifteen years but, like all horsemen, being where horses were kept, smelling them, listening to them eat, was salve for the soul.

The liveryman's name was Reg Lee. He was in his forties but looked older and drank too much. He also had a paunch that prevented him from seeing anything below his belt without using a mirror. Once he'd had a wife, a 'breed woman as tall and handsome as a breedy mare. One morning Reg had gotten out of bed, and she was not there. That had been almost ten years earlier.

As Hugh settled against a cribbed corral stringer looking at some horses, the liveryman came along sucking his teeth. "Nice night," he said.

Hugh nodded about that. There was not much of a moon, but it was pleasantly warm without any wind.

Reg leaned on the corral. "Them damned animals stand around here eatin' their heads off. It's hard makin' a livin' off somethin' that eats all the time."

22

Hugh nodded about that, too, then the liveryman said something that caused Pepperdine to look around at him. "That young buck you got apprenticed to you—the blacksmith's helper said he seen him get the tar punched out of him in a brawl up in San Luis a year or so back."

Hugh eyed the other man. "Fightin' a gambler?"

"Nope. Some cowboy."

Hugh turned back to regarding the horses, and by the time he was ready to leave Reg had been called into his barn by someone needing a horse cared for.

He slow-paced his way back up toward the lighted harness shop. Besides getting euchreed by that damned weasel-eyed Davy Barber, he had a brawler on his hands.

When he walked in George was oiling the underside of the saddle skirt. He'd already scrubbed it clean. He glanced up then down again. Hugh thought it had to be about nine o'clock, which made a hell of a long workday. He owned a watch but had stopped carrying it years ago because it was never running when he looked at it. The reason it was never running was because he never remembered to wind it.

He watched the youth work. He had no wasted motions. For someone who'd never worked leather before he took to it like a duck takes to water, and that was fine. Hugh stepped outside to jettison his cud and returned as George was lightly sponging a sheep pelt. Hugh said, "Now then, when you get it lightly glued, you'll want to take shears and cut the pelt real low all the way around, otherwise when you sew it the wool will come through the holes with the thread."

George did not look up.

Hugh got a fresh cud settled and continued to lean, watching the youth work. Across the road someone

23

banging on Rusty Morton's old piano made a lot of noise but very little music. That was about the only sound until the northbound evening stage rattled up through town, late as usual, and turned into the corralyard for a change of horses before continuing upcountry.

Hugh waited until his apprentice had locked the skirt between the jaws of the sewing horse and was expertly twisting the flax thread on a trouser leg before pulling it through a ball of beeswax then headed for his own room off the back of the shop.

The lad would make out all right. He wasn't going to get much sleep tonight, but that was his own fault.

Before retiring, Hugh visited the outhouse and on his way back paused to look at a sky speckled with little diamond-chip stars, spit out his chew, and blow out a big breath.

One thing was as sure as the fact that gawd had made little green apples. His days of routine living were unlikely to return to that comfortable schedule as long as he had George Jefferson working with him.

Tomorrow would be the fifth day, and while Hugh was not only satisfied with the way the lad worked, was in fact even a little awed by the way he picked things up, unless something happened between them soon he was going to spend eight months working with a mute. Even that wasn't altogether worrisome, but those stories he'd heard about George were.

Hugh had been involved in his share of violence over the years, but grizzled now and less prone to real anger, he did not like the idea of having someone around him who might explode at any moment.

He lowered his eyes from the sky, called Davy Barber a harsh name, and returned to his room. Light showed under the door where the lad was stitching that old saddle skirt.

CHAPTER 4

A Surprise

IN THE MORNING GEORGE HAD ALREADY BEEN TO THE cafe and was back to work by the time Hugh emerged from his room. They exchanged a nod. Hugh dropped a fistful of ground coffee beans into the old pot, filled it with water, and fired up the stove.

There was a hint of changing weather to the morning, but by afternoon it would be warm again with a summer-blue sky up there.

When the cowman came for his saddle skirt Hugh nodded from where he was crafting the new saddle and left it up to his apprentice to take the money and hand over the skirt. But he listened carefully as the old rancher critically examined the work and complimented George about it. After the cowman had departed, another satisfied customer, Hugh straightened up and said, "What time did you get to bed last night?"

"Don't own a timepiece," the youth replied, and went after the coal-oil bottle to get beeswax off his hands. He had his back to Hugh when he said, "There's somethin' I got to do today. Is that all right?"

As far as the work was concerned Hugh had no objections. "Anythin' you need help at?" he asked, and got a head shake.

"No. I'll be back when I can."

After the youth had dropped a floppy old hat atop his mass of brown hair and left the shop, Hugh got himself a cup of coffee and was standing with his backside to the little stove when James McGregor walked in, jerking his head rearward. "Where's he goin' with that gun?"

Hugh stared. "What gun? He walked out of here not ten minutes ago an' he wasn't wearin' a gun."

"Well, he's wearin' one now. I saw him walkin' toward the lower end of town with a shellbelt around his belly and a holstered gun on his leg."

Hugh stood like stone holding the coffee cup. "If his back was to you it could have been—"

"Hugh, nothin' wrong with my eyesight. It was your lad, an' he was wearin' a six-gun."

Hugh put the cup down very carefully, brushed past his old friend, and stood in the center of the plankwalk squinting southward. There was no sign of his apprentice. As he turned slowly back into the shop McGregor said, "No sign of him?"

"No."

"Did you give him the day off?"

"Yeah. He said he had somethin' he had to do today."

McGregor filled a cup from the pot and seemed lost in thought for a long time before speaking again. "You don't suppose he's goin' to rob a stage or maybe catch someone ridin' alone out there, do you?"

Hugh threw up his arms. "I don't suppose anythin', but I'll tell you one thing: When he comes back this evenin' we're goin' to set down and talk like a couple of Dutch uncles."

McGregor let that pass. "Maybe you'd ought to go down an' tell Joe Fogarty. The lad's been in trouble before, Hugh. Sure as hell you don't want to get dragged into somethin' he might do."

Pepperdine turned that over in his mind and decided it

might not be a bad idea even if it got his apprentice into trouble, or maybe prevented him from getting into trouble, so he jerked his head for the gunsmith to accompany him and struck out for the Sheridan jailhouse.

They were in for the surprise of their lives.

Joe Fogarty was staring at the ceiling when they walked in. He brought his head down, looked longest at Hugh, gently wagged his head as he fidgeted in his chair, and spoke. "I saw your apprentice ridin' north out of town, but not up the roadway. He went west a mile before turnin' north."

Hugh looked around for a chair. "He told me he had to do somethin' today, so I let him go."

Fogarty's gaze drifted to the gunsmith then moved slowly to the gun rack with its padlocked chain running through the trigger guards of a number of weapons. He nodded toward the little potbellied stove. "Coffee's hot if you want some."

Neither of the older men left their chairs or spoke.

Fogarty leaned back, considered the ceiling briefly, then shot up to his feet. "Take a little walk with me," he said, and did not wait for a response as he put on his hat and crossed to the door and walked out of the office.

McGregor was scowling. "Something's wrong," he muttered as he arose. Hugh said nothing; he was beginning to get a bad feeling. Fogarty was acting as though something had happened serious enough to make him appear different toward his old friends.

Outside roadway traffic was light, but pedestrian traffic was heavy for Sheridan as the three men walked northward as far as a little smelly dogtrot and emerged in the eastside alley where a surprised dog was reconnoitering a trash bin and fled at sight of the two-

27

legged creatures.

Dr. Pohl's residence, with its pair of spare rooms for very ill people, backed to the alley with a small picket fence around an intervening yard where someone had been valiantly struggling to raise pink and red geraniums.

West of the yard and across the alley was what could once have been a carriage shed or where someone had stored firewood. It now served as Henry Pohl's embalming shed, and as Marshal Fogarty approached it the unique aroma of formaldehyde was noticeable.

Hugh looked at the big lawman's back with a frown, but McGregor was totally impassive, even though he did not feel disinterested. It was simply that James McGregor rarely showed much expression and even more rarely laughed or smiled.

Fogarty knocked lightly on the shed door. From beyond it a voice both older men recognized as belonging to Dr. Pohl answered.

"Who is it?"

"Joe Fogarty."

"Come in."

The shed had no window now, although it clearly had once had one before it had been boarded up. Darkness was kept at bay by coal-oil lamps: three of them around the room and one large lamp with an opaque, unadorned glass shade.

When Fogarty stepped inside, McGregor finally showed some expression. His friend did, too, but a more pronounced expression as Fogarty addressed the physician.

"The lad left town about an hour ago, Henry. Hugh came along, and after thinkin' things over I figured he deserved to see what we got."

Henry Pohl's original scowl of disapproval when two unannounced men entered his embalming shed was still in place, even after Fogarty's statement, but he reached for a towel and was drying his hands on it as he said, "I suppose so. Hugh anyway." He approached the table, which was somewhat higher than ordinary tables, and lifted a length of old, soiled canvas.

Hugh's breath stopped in his throat. McGregor's eyes steadily widened. Dr. Pohl said, "Beautiful, wasn't she?"

No one replied.

The corpse was a woman. Perhaps in life she had been somewhere in her early forties, but even now she looked younger. She had hair as black as a crow's wing with a few strands of silver over each ear. Her features, which had once been golden tan, were flawless even in death.

McGregor recovered before Hugh. "Who was she? I never saw her before, sure as hell not in town."

Joe Fogarty replied quietly while gazing at the table. "She wasn't from around here. Her name was Helen Jefferson."

Hugh's gaze lifted slowly to the lawman's face. "Jefferson?"

Fogarty nodded. "Yeah. Your apprentice's mother."

"What happened to her? She don't look like she died yesterday."

Henry Pohl was using the towel again, although his hands were no longer damp. He seemed unwilling to speak, so Marshal Fogarty did it for him.

"Pneumonia. James?"

McGregor answered shortly. "Yes."

"Remember I told you about cracking my carbine stock prying rocks off a grave up in the foothills?"

29

"I remember."

"She was in it. I took a couple of men up there yesterday in a wagon, opened the grave, brought back the body all wrapped in yards of white cloth, and there she is."

Hugh looked for something to sit on. There was a little bench nailed to the north wall, but he did not approach it. He groaned, looking from one of them to the other. "Why'n hell did you dig her up, Joe? Sure as I'm standin' here that's where the lad went this morning. He's goin' to find the grave open, his mother gone, and wagon tracks comin' back to town."

James McGregor summed it up bluntly. "He's wearin' a gun, and all three of us know he'll use it."

Dr. Pohl stopped wiping his hands. At a time like this Henry Pohl reacted as just about everyone did in the community. He looked steadily at Marshal Fogarty, whose job was to uphold the law and also to explain events.

His explanation was valid, but all it accomplished was to increase the anxiety of the two older men. "All I knew was that someone'd been buried up there awhile back. It's my job to know why people die. I had no idea who she was or even that it was a woman until Henry an' I unrolled her out of yards of that white cloth."

"How did you know her name was Helen Jefferson?" Hugh asked.

Fogarty fished in a shirt pocket, wordlessly handed Hugh a crumpled slip of paper, and exchanged a long look with the doctor. He gently inclined his head, and as Henry replaced the gray canvas over the face of the corpse, Hugh haltingly read aloud from the paper in his hand.

"If you would have told me, Mother, I would have

30

made it right. George."

McGregor's brows met in the middle. "What does that mean?"

Henry Pohl answered slowly. "Joe's going up to San Luis to find out."

Hugh snorted. "That's not nearly as important as findin' that damned kid with the gun. Joe, if he tracks the wagon back to town—if you got it from Reg Lee he's goin' to find out it was you that dug his mother up."

Fogarty nodded. He and Henry had gone through all this late last night. In fact, this was what he'd been preoccupied about when McGregor and Pepperdine had walked into the jailhouse office this morning.

"He's goin' to have to wait. I'm leavin' town on the northbound coach in about half an hour. He's goin' to have to wait until I get back, an' I got no idea when that'll be. Maybe tomorrow, if I can get all the answers I need up there, an' maybe not for a couple more days."

McGregor made a dour comment. "You better pray he don't know you're on that stage."

Fogarty turned. "He's somewhere out yonder. There's no way he could know that."

Henry Pohl said, "What I'd give a lot to know is what the note means. If she had told him what? One thing I'm sure of is that she was sick, and she knew it. Maybe George knew it, too, but regardless of that, that piece of paper hints to me there was somethin' she wouldn't tell the boy."

Joe nodded. "An' she took it to the grave with her." He frowned. "Why did he go up there today?"

McGregor, who knew something about that kind of anguish, replied. "Because that was where he buried her. It was the last place they were together. Joe, if you

31

can't understand somethin' like that then you've never lost someone you loved with your whole heart."

No one said a word until Henry Pohl moved to blow down the chimneys of his lamps. When the four of them were back outside in sunlight the doctor nodded brusquely and crossed the alley to the rear of his house, leaving the two older men and Marshal Fogarty to slow-pace their way back through the dogtrot as far as the front of the jailhouse, where Hugh halted. He said, "Well now, we got a dynamite stick with a lighted short fuse out there somewhere, an' by this evenin' he'll be comin' back."

Fogarty was watching roadway traffic when he replied to that. "He's only got one place to go when he can't find me."

Hugh fished for his cut plug. "Anyone else in town know any of this goddamned mess you got us into, Joe?"

Fogarty reddened. "I didn't get us into anything. I just did my duty as a lawman. No; as far as I know only you two, Henry, and I know about the woman and your lad's relationship to her."

Hugh stated an obvious fact. "It'd be best if it stayed that way."

Fogarty walked into his office and returned in a few moments to head for the corralyard. Up ahead of him McGregor and Pepperdine were already turning into the harness shop. When Fogarty strode past he did not even look in, which wouldn't have made much difference because McGregor and Pepperdine had passed on through the shop to Hugh's lean-to living quarters where he kept a bottle of malt whiskey.

As McGregor held his glass steady to be filled, Hugh said, "If I could get my hands on Davy Barber right this

32

minute I'd slit both his ears and yank his arms through them."

James wasn't thinking of Barber, nor even George Jefferson. He was thinking of that note. As he settled back in a rickety chair he said, "If she told him what? An' somethin' else, Hugh. Did she die up there in the foothills, or did the lad bring her down there to bury her, and that don't seem likely since he was a workin' range rider. Nope, she was more'n likely campin' up there. I got a notion to close the shop an' ride up yonder and poke around."

Hugh downed his whiskey, ran a soiled sleeve across his eyes, and blew out a flammatory breath before growling at his friend. "You're crazy. You show up anywhere near that grave an' that boy's goin' to blow holes in your carcass a man could drive a wagon through."

McGregor was stung. "What the hell are you talkin about? He barely even knows me."

"That won't matter. James, I been around that feller for close to a couple of weeks, an' if there's one thing I've figured out it's that deep down, he's got somethin' like a bed of coals in his guts. . . . He wouldn't have to know you or me or anyone else today, not when he sees someone's robbed his mother's grave. You know the stories; how he challenges folks to fight."

McGregor looked for a place to put his empty jolt glass, settled for an upended horseshoe keg Hugh used for a stand beside his old iron cot, put the glass down, and stood up. "I told you not to get into any deal with Davy Barber."

Hugh also rose. "If you knew how to play a mouth harp you could set that to music. You say it every time we meet."

"Well, it's true, isn't it?"

"Yes, you old haggis eater, it's true. Now shut up about it."

By the time they had walked back through the shop to the front roadway, McGregor's irritability had diminished. He saw dust far up the north roadway and jutted his jaw Indian-fashion. "I hope he finds whatever he wants to know up in San Luis and gets back here by tomorrow, because I got a hunch we're goin' to have a real ring-tailed roarer on our hands when the lad comes back."

Hugh watched his old friend striding in the direction of the gun shop. *We* got a ring-tailed roarer on *our* hands. . . .

It made all the difference in the world in a man's life when he had friends like James McGregor.

Even if the old screwt was raised on dead meat rolled in oatmeal and stuffed inside a sheep's entrails like sausage.

They'd once had a furious argument about that. McGregor had said it wasn't dead meat rolled in oatmeal, but he did admit there was a lot of oatmeal in it, and it had indeed been stuffed into sheep's entrails. It was called haggis, and although he'd tasted it as a youngster, he hadn't even remembered the stuff for more than fifty years.

Like most of their arguments, no one emerged with a clear victory.

CHAPTER 5

A Very Long Day

BEFORE THE SUN SANK, HUGH LOOKED UP EVERY TIME someone's shadow fell across the front window. A couple of times, when someone walked in, his heart skipped a beat; but each time it was a customer. The last time it was the local stage-line manager, Silas Browning, wearing his oversized hat and looking like someone who'd just encountered a bad odor, which was his normal expression.

He was a small man, without many teeth, and the ones he still had did not seem to mesh. He was old but no one knew how old. He was also sinewy, with squinty little pale eyes. He had an annoying habit of sniffing, probably unaware that he was doing it most of the time.

When he came in out of the late-day shadows, Hugh groaned under his breath, dried his hands, and waited. Silas stalked to the counter, hung his arms atop it, and said, "They busted my running-W this morning. Can you fix it?"

Hugh's reply dripped with sarcasm. "How can I answer that until I see it, Silas?"

"It's pretty bad."

Hugh was beginning to suspect the rig was more than just "pretty bad." It was probably torn beyond repair, and old Silas, who was tighter-fisted than even Pete Donner at the bank, wanted a new one made. "Bring it in," he told the older man.

Silas's perpetually narrowed eyes went around the room and back to Hugh. "How much would a new one

35

cost? Remember now, I give you all my business."

Hugh nodded about that; the reason he got all the stage company's business was because the only other harness works in the country was twenty miles south, down at Bordenton.

"Seven dollars."

Silas's little eyes blinked wide for a moment. "Seven dollars! I can reuse the same hobbles, for crissake, that leaves only the ring-halter an' the lines, an' I can use ropes for the lines."

Hugh hung one ham on the worktable before speaking again. "An' the surcingle, Silas, with side-rings for the lines. It takes time to sew all that doubled leather."

"You got that beanpole of a kid Davy Barber left behind when he trailed south a week or so ago."

Hugh hadn't known Barber had left the country. He had known Barber would leave, and he probably should have suspected he'd already left, but he perched there gazing at the wizened old gummer inside his huge hat as he said, "Barber's gone?"

"I just told you he left some time back. Now then, everyone around town knows he apprenticed that boy out to you. Apprentices work for beans. He can do the sewin' and cut the cost way down."

Hugh stood up and went over where he'd been working on the new saddle. "Seven dollars, Silas."

Browning made his sniffing noise. "That's highway robbery." He was poised to say more, but the look on Pepperdine's face kept him from it. As he turned toward the door he said, "I'll send it down in a day or two. If the damned idiot who was usin' it knew up from down he'd never have let the horse he was tryin' to break from runnin' get plumb to the end of the lines before he

36

dumped him."

Hugh resumed work on the new saddle. He was positioning the rigging, something he took great pains about because, although most saddles were rigged full double, Hugh knew after years of experience that full double rigging caused more sores than any other kind. He set his front rigging far enough back so that the rigging did not come in close, where an animal's front legs moved back and forth.

He was concentrating on his work and didn't know he had a customer until the man at the counter cleared his throat. It was Rusty Morton from across the road at the saloon. Rusty didn't own a horse nor even a buggy. In fact, except for an occasional dull day when he was bored, he rarely visited Hugh's shop.

Rusty looked around. "Where's the lad?"

Hugh straightened up. "He's not here. Why?"

"Just wondered. He braided me a watch fob. Prettiest piece of flat plaiting I ever saw. I come over to pay him and tell how good a job he did."

Hugh said, "Leave the money on the counter. I'll see that he gets it."

As the moon-faced barman was counting out coins, he also said, "Davy should have took him south when he left. That lad's got some real skills. Next time you're over remind me to show you that fob." He placed the coins on the counter and smiled. "Can you imagine any woman in her right mind marryin' Davy?"

Hugh's brows drew down a little in bafflement. "He got married? Where you'd hear that?"

"A traveling peddler left an Arizona newspaper in the saloon. I saw it on the front page. Married some widow-woman named Blake." Morton looked rueful. "She's in for the lesson of her life; Davy don't shave nor bathe nor change his britches until the buzzards start circlin' every time he rides out."

Morton walked back across the roadway. Hugh watched until he disappeared beyond the spindle doors of his saloon, then went scowlingly back to work on the rigging. What he should probably have asked, or Rusty Morton should have said, was what the date was on that Arizona newspaper, because Hugh had heard a rumor a year or so back that Davy Barber already had a wife. But that didn't have to mean anything; if a man wanted to listen he could hear anything, even the date of the Second Coming. But as Rusty had implied, this lady was in for the lesson of her life, whether she was number two or not. Unless, of course, she was cut from the same cloth, and to Hugh Pepperdine's knowledge, there was no such a female, widowed or otherwise.

He was unaware that he'd come to have such bad thoughts about Barber that, no matter what, he wouldn't have been able to think otherwise about him.

Shadows in the roadway made less of a difference than the appearance of oncoming dusk made inside the shop. Hugh had to light two lamps to continue working on the saddle, although visibility outside was still fairly good.

He was satisfied with the fitting of the rigging and was placing it flat out on the worktable when James appeared in the doorway to say, "He's comin' up this way from the lower end of town. I'll bet you a new hat he got all he wanted to know out of Reg Lee."

Hugh forgot about the rigging. He hadn't been more than indifferently concentrating on it anyway. He shed his apron and joined the gunsmith out front.

James made another observation. "He's not wearin' the gun."

38

Hugh stepped back inside with McGregor following him. They waited a long time before McGregor got impatient and approached the doorway again. Without turning back he called to Pepperdine. "He just came out of the jailhouse."

Hugh sighed. The sequence they'd theorized about was being proven true; George had tracked the wagon back to town, down to Lee's barn, and had got the information out of the liveryman about who had been driving that rig.

They were standing near the stove when the lanky youth walked in. His face showed nothing, and although he nodded he said nothing. He would have walked through to his room but Hugh caught him by the arm and swung him around. "We're goin' to palaver," he told the youth as he released his arm. "An' maybe you'd be right if you told me it wasn't none of my business where you been today and why you went up there, but George, as long as you're stayin' here with me, I figure I got a right to know, because if the damned sky falls on you, boy, some of it's goin' to also fall on me."

The youth's tawny eyes did not leave Pepperdine's face. He said, "Where's the marshal?"

"Out of town," McGregor answered.

"When'll he be back?"

"Don't rightly know."

George flicked a glance at the gunsmith but returned his gaze to Hugh and kept it there as he spoke again. "Why did you say just now that I'd been—up there?"

Hugh wasn't aware that he'd said it, but he didn't shy away from a blunt answer either. "Because we know where you went. We know a little more, too." Hugh paused for a moment while he thought of ways to arrange his next words. The lanky youth was looking directly at him from eyes that had no spark in them, dull eyes. Hugh started up again. "I'm a lot older'n you are. Whatever's burnin' you up inside, I've been through it, too. Boy, you're good around the shop. Better'n I expected. But before we keep up our arrangement we got to thrash out a few things."

"I got nothin' to say until the marshal gets back," the lad retorted, and would have moved again but this time when Hugh grabbed his arm the grip was like steel. Nor did he release the arm as he'd done before.

"Maybe you don't have anythin' to say, George, but I sure as hell have."

"Let go of my arm."

Hugh acted deaf. "We're goin' to start at the beginning." He'd barely got the words out when the lanky youth attacked him with big, bony fists. Hugh was struck twice, but when the third fist was fired he was already swinging the boy by the arm. The fist missed Hugh but nearly caught McGregor before Hugh got both arms locked around the boy's chest in a viselike grip. He grunted as he reared back, lifted George off the floor, then simultaneously leaned forward and released his grip, slamming George to the floor.

The boy wasn't injured, but he rolled slowly up into a sitting position and put both hands over his face. When he spoke through his fingers the words sounded unsteady. "I'll kill you."

Hugh's answer was sharp. "You're not goin' to kill anybody. Get up on your feet, an' if you try that again, I'll peel the hide off you an inch at a time. Get up!"

McGregor leaned to hoist George upright. He managed it as though the boy were weightless. Both McGregor and Hugh stared. Tears were running down both George's cheeks. He didn't look dangerous, he

40

looked pathetic.

Hugh let go a loud, rattling sigh, walked up to the front of the shop, locked the door, and walked back. McGregor was talking to the lad. ". . . think you're the only one who's lost someone. But you're luckier'n I was when I lost my wife. I didn't have anyone to talk to. You do have. Boy, get it out of you because I can tell you for a fact that if you don't, it's goin' to ruin your whole damned life an' maybe get you killed. We know about you pitchin' into some cowboy and gettin' the whey knocked out of you and about you challengin' some tinhorn up in San Luis to a fight in the roadway."

Hugh was tenderly exploring a cheek where he'd been struck. "Come along," he told them both, and led the way to his lean-to room. There he pointed to chairs, and George approached one but did not sit down. Neither did McGregor. Hugh shrugged, sat on a little stool, and eyed the youth. "What'd you want to see the marshal about?" he asked, and when George was mopping both cheeks with a cuff as though he had not heard the question, Hugh said, "It was his job to investigate the grave, boy. He didn't want to open it any more'n I would have. Or James here. She's up in Dr. Pohl's shed. This time she'll be buried Christianlike and decent. . . . George? Damn you, boy, when I ask you a question you answer me. You understand?"

Hugh arose from his stool, hands fisted at his side. McGregor scowled at his old friend. Hugh loosened a little and unknotted his fists, ran a set of bent fingers through his hair, and turned away to hunt for the bottle of malt whiskey. He hadn't been this upset in years.

As he was getting the bottle, McGregor asked George a question. "When did she die?"

He got an answer. "A week back."

41

"How do you know that?"

"Because after Mr. Pepperdine got to snoring I snuck out and borrowed a horse down at the liverybarn and rode up where she was camped."

"Go on, boy. Let me tell you something. We're your friends. Maybe the only ones you got. Get on with it; was she sick?"

". . . She was dead. . . . I knew she was sick. She said it was just a cold, but it sounded worse'n any cold I ever had. She'd sit by the fire with me an' we'd talk. All I knew was that she wouldn't tell me everything even when I kept on asking. She'd hug me, and sometimes she'd cry."

"How long did she camp up there?"

"Since early last spring when I wrote her a letter sayin' I'd got hired on by a man named Davy Barber. She come down here, and once when I was ridin' out she was standin' in a little clearing smiling like she used to do when I was little."

"How'd she manage?"

"I bought grub and took it up there to her."

"Didn't Mr. Barber know?"

"I'd sneak away in the night like I did after I come to work here at the harness shop. He didn't know. But there was something . . ."

Hugh was standing in lamp shadow holding the whiskey bottle when he said, "What—something?"

"I don't know. When we'd talk about my work she'd sit there huggin' her knees and lookin' into the fire like I wasn't even there. . . . Sometimes when I was little she'd do that, too. My mother was a third 'breed In'ian. Sometimes she seemed more'n a third."

Hugh looked at the bottle in his fist, put it on the upended horseshoe keg beside his bed, and sat down on the edge of the cot. In a soft voice he said, "George, why didn't you get her to come down to Sheridan? Livin' in the foothills like an In'ian last spring when it rained a lot wasn't a good thing, for her or anyone."

"She didn't want to come down here. She didn't know anyone. There wasn't no money. She said she liked it up there in the quiet and all. But I knew she was sick. I told her there was a doctor in Sheridan. She'd smile about that and start talkin' about when I was little in our shack out west of San Luis."

Hugh and McGregor exchanged a long look; then Hugh removed the cap from the bottle and held it out. "One swallow, boy. Just one."

George took one swallow and probably wouldn't have taken another one anyway, but Hugh took back the bottle and handed it to the gunsmith. He said, "That'll make you sleep, George. Have you eaten lately?"

"Supper last night."

"Now then, go to your room and sleep. In the morning we'll talk some more."

CHAPTER 6

Hugh's Dilemma

FOR HALF AN HOUR AFTER GEORGE HAD DEPARTED THE two older men sipped whiskey and carried on a desultory conversation that did not really advance their understanding at all but which helped them define a few things. One had to do with that gun James had seen the lad wearing. He thought George had the gun hidden somewhere, probably away from the shop, outside it but not very far from it, because between the time the lad

43

had departed from the harness works and the time McGregor had seen him walking southward wearing the gun couldn't have been more than about ten minutes.

And Hugh had been puzzling over something since they'd seen the dead woman in Henry Pohl's shed. "Joe said her name was Helen Jefferson. All right; he knew the lad's name, so if she was his mother her name would most likely be the same. But there was nothin' in that note George buried with her that mentioned the name Helen."

McGregor sipped, thought, and came up with a question of his own. "How did he know she was the lad's mother?"

They did not pursue either of these topics because both were tired and it had been a long day. Hugh let his friend out the front door, relocked it, and went back to bed down. Sleep came easily as it had been doing the last ten years or so. But when Hugh awakened in the morning, the answers they'd got, plus the riddles they had no answers to, were again uppermost in his mind.

He went out front to fire up the stove and put the coffeepot atop it. The shop was cold, the front door was still locked, and there was not a sound from the other back room.

With mounting anxiety he went back there and rapped on the door. There was no answer, so he rolled all his knuckles across wood a second time, then gripped the latch, lifted it, and looked in.

George was not there. An imprint showed that someone had been lying atop the blankets, but when he crossed over and put his hand on them the blankets were cold.

He straightened up to look around. The bedroll and warbag were still there. In fact, his initial worry—that the lad had departed in the night with all his gatherings—was not substantiated by what he saw.

He returned to the shop, got a cup of coffee, and went around behind the counter to stare at the rigging on the worktable where he'd left it yesterday. Some people ran to friends to unburden themselves of their worries, and some went to brood in the company of John Barleycorn. Pepperdine was the kind that lost himself in his work. He left the cup on the counter and busied himself fitting the rigging, fixing it in place with brass screws, making minute adjustments here and there, then critically testing it for fit and hang before going back to the swell covering to make certain that, now that it was dry, the fit was wrinkle-free and snug.

An hour later, when he was marking tin patterns for the fenders and stirrup leathers, Silas Browning appeared carrying a wooden crate. He upended it atop the counter. Hugh went over to finger through the scraps of leather. Neither of them had said a word, not even the customary "good morning."

Hugh shook his head. He could patch the running-W, but it would never again be as strong as it originally had been. Since the sole function of a running-W was to pit human strength against the strength of a horse so that the human could win, it had to be very strong.

He looked up from the pile of scraps. Old Silas immediately picked up a cheekpiece of the ring-halter. "Wouldn't take a man fifteen minutes to restitch that. And here now, this—"

"Silas, it's not worth what it'd cost you," Hugh announced, as he began dumping the scraps back into the box.

Browning's little watery eyes looked malevolent as he regarded the harnessmaker. "The lad could repair it,

Hugh. That is, when he gets back."

Pepperdine saw the spiteful expression. "Gets back from where?"

"From wherever he went on the mail coach last night. Up north somewhere."

Hugh leaned on the counter, studying the old man. "Last night?"

"Yes, last night. The only stage I send out after dark is the mail coach. Usually along about ten, eleven o'clock. I never liked that part of the mail contract, an' I told 'em that. There's nothin' in a bunch of letters that couldn't wait for daylight. They told me if I wanted the contract I'd have to do what the government—"

"Where up north, Silas?"

The old man made a sniffing sound. "How would I know? He walked into the yard, asked how much to let him ride on the stage, an' paid me. Maybe only as far as San Luis, maybe all the way up to the spur tracks where they take the bags of mail the rest of the way to Denver. He didn't say, an' I didn't ask." Silas's spiteful look deepened. "You didn't know, eh? I figured you wouldn't. Now then, when he gets back about this here leather harness . . ."

"Leave it," Hugh said. "Just leave it. I'll see what can be done."

"When?"

Hugh's face darkened. "The other day you said you wasn't in a hurry."

"Well, no, but a man likes to have the rig on hand if he suddenly needs it, don't he?"

Hugh's baleful, troubled gaze froze Silas's malevolent smile in place. After a moment the old man readjusted his huge old hat, nodded, and headed for the doorway. Out there he said, "All right. Whenever you or

46

the lad can get to it."

When Hugh got over to the gun shop McGregor was deep in conversation with a swarthy, dark man with a mouth like a bear trap and fish-steady, dark eyes. He was Pete Donner, born Pierre Donnier, the head of the Sheridan Bank and Trust Company, whose brick building was opposite the harness works and southward a short distance.

James and Pete nodded to Hugh. Donner was hefting a spanking new nickel-plated Lightning Colt. He faced Hugh with it as he said, "Did you ever use one of these?"

Hugh hadn't. They hadn't been around much during Hugh's period of gun-wearing, and when he finally saw them the scornful comment among rangemen was that they'd been made for women, especially if they were nickel plated. They were double-action revolvers, which was one advantage over the old single-action six-guns, and they were smaller. Pete Donner said, "The Pinkertons carry them. That's what made me think I'd maybe ought to buy one to keep in the bank."

Hugh waited patiently until Donner had purchased the gun and departed, then he told James about George's disappearance and got a wide-eyed look. "He went to San Luis sure as hell," McGregor exclaimed. "And Joe's still up there. You reckon he knows that and went up there to settle with Fogarty after all?"

Hugh considered another of those little double-action Colts lying on the counter. "The idea came to me, James. By now he's up there. We got no telegraph in Sheridan, or we could maybe warn Joe."

McGregor also gazed at the new revolver then gently put it back in his gun rack over near the east wall before speaking again. "Nothing much a man can do now.

47

Someone could go up there, an' by then if ambushin' Fogarty was on the lad's mind, he would have done it."

Hugh felt for his cut plug, but the taste was less than satisfactory because he hadn't had breakfast yet, so he returned the plug to a pocket and jettisoned the fresh cud in a battered old brass spittoon. "He didn't seem to want Joe as much after we all talked last night. That's the feelin' I got anyway. How about you?"

McGregor returned to lean on the counter. "I had the same impression." He raised his eyes to the taller man's face. "Maybe that's not why he went up there."

"Maybe. What did he go up there for, an' why'n hell did he sneak out like that? Last night we was closer to bein' friends than we ever been."

McGregor could provide no answers. Hugh ambled down to the cafe, where business was slackening off, ordered, and sat hunched at the counter, staring at the pie table where two shiny flies were trying to figure out how to get inside the glass bowl that had been placed in an inverted position over half a degenerating apple pie.

The cafeman, addicted to cloth slippers because years earlier he'd frozen his feet while cowboying for a big outfit up in Montana, was overweight, somewhat slovenly, and perhaps as a result of constant pain from his feet, had a surly disposition.

Hugh ignored him as he ate. Later he couldn't remember who else had been having breakfast the same time he was. Nor did it matter.

Later in the day, about midafternoon, one of Silas Browning's drivers, a man named Jack Carpenter, entered the shop. Carpenter had a wife and children down in Bordenton along with a nagging brother-in-law who was forever bracing Carpenter because he drank.

He also chewed, which was entirely respectable. So

48

was drinking, up to a point. Jack had passed that point a long time ago, but he had one of the best excuses any habitual drinker had ever come up with: Driving stages year-round was a miserable job, especially during the winters when it got down to zero and below and hung there for days on end, cold enough to freeze the *chingalees* off a brass monkey. The only way a man could keep the cold off the outside of his carcass was to bundle up like a bear. The only way he could keep it from congealing his insides was to nip on a bottle of popskull as he herded his horses along.

Hugh and Jack had been acquaintances for years, but this morning, when Carpenter came in looking tired, Hugh's interest quickened. But he went through the rangecountry ritual of etiquette. First he asked how theweather was, and Jack replied predictably. "Ain't been bad lately, but we're goin' to have an early winter colder'n a witch's bosom."

"How are the roads?"

"Like a damned washboard half way up to San Luis, worse beyond, with washouts an—"

"You just come in off a run, Jack?"

"Yep, and now I can go home and set for a couple of days. Silas don't like that but—"

"The mail run last night, Jack?"

"Yep."

"Have a passenger, did you?"

Carpenter leaned on the counter, eyeing Pepperdine. He knew about the apprentice. "Your lad. He sat up on the high seat with me. Sure don't talk a lot, does he?"

"No, not much. Did he say why he was goin' up there?"

Carpenter's perpetually narrowed eyes widened a little. "Well, you knew, didn't you? He used to live up

49

there. Somewhere northwest of town. He was goin'
back to look for something. Didn't he tell you that?"

Hugh lied like a trooper. "Yeah, he told me. But like
you said, he don't talk much. He didn't tell me exactly
what he was lookin' for."

"Some old pictures an' some odds and ends. At least
that's what he told me, but he didn't act like he was real
right in the head."

Hugh's relief was enormous. He said, "Wait here a
minute," and winked as he went to the back room and
returned with his bottle of malt whiskey.

Carpenter's eyes brightened. He settled into a more
comfortable position against the counter and sipped
from the bottle. The tired look diminished; Carpenter's
color improved. He held the bottle at arm's length,
reading the label. As he took another sip, he said, "If
Rusty'd carry stuff like this he'd have more customers.
Where'd you get it?"

"Off a freighter who passed through last spring. He
told me someone over east a hunnert miles or so made it
for the carriage trade."

Carpenter screwed the cap on and blew out a fiery
breath. "He was tellin' the gospel truth, wasn't he?
Well, I killed enough time, the southbound for
Bordenton will be hitched up by now. Thanks, Hugh. It
was nice visitin' with you."

Pepperdine returned to his work with a sense of relief.
Later when Hank Dennis, the proprietor of the big local
mercantile business across the road and south of the
cafe, came in with a set of cloth braces that had torn
buttonholes where they fastened to his trousers, the
whiskey bottle was still on the counter. Dennis, a
married man with a two-thirds grown daughter, was
another hardshell Baptist but not as obnoxious a one as

50

Silas Browning was. He nevertheless gave the offending bottle a walleyed look then held out the suspenders and explained what had to be done to them.

Hugh discreetly swept the bottle out of sight below the counter with one hand while taking the braces with the other hand. "When do you need them?" he asked the balding, portly storekeeper.

"I got another pair; in fact, I got twenty new sets at the store, but these here ones—"

"How about before closin' time today?"

Dennis looked surprised. Hugh had a reputation in town and out over the countryside for never finishing anything until he was damned good and ready to do so. "I'd be obliged," Dennis said. "They're my favorites. Bendin' over a lot is awful hard on buttons and buttonholes."

Hugh was sympathetic. "I know. A man's got to depend on his britches stayin' up. Come back in a couple hours."

Dennis returned to the roadway marveling at old Pepperdine's vastly improved disposition. He acted almost as though a big worry had just been lifted off his shoulders.

Hank was right, and Hugh finished the braces in record time then hastened over to the gun shop where McGregor was firing up a little container beneath one of his silver melting pots. There were six molds lined up waiting for the liquid silver to fill them. They had scallopped edges that indicated the finished products were to be either rosettes for headstalls or conchos for saddles.

McGregor threw Hugh a dour look, and Hugh waved a hand. "Get on with it like I wasn't here. It's nothin' that won't keep anyway."

51

CHAPTER 7

The Advent of Change

THE FOLLOWING AFTERNOON TWO EVENTS THAT happened almost simultaneously gave relief to Hugh Pepperdine as well as additional cause for anxiety.

The first event was the arrival of a large, mop-headed cowman who ran livestock west and south of Sheridan whose name was Buster Henning. He was the man Hugh had been making the saddle for.

Henning was an outgoing person, good-natured and unassuming, although he was reputedly wealthy, and everyone knew for a fact that he kept four riders year-round and during the working season had as many as ten. His grazing land adjoined Davy Barber's territory.

Henning wanted to know how his saddle was coming along, and Hugh took all the time that was required to explain what he had done and why he had done it. Working with leather was Hugh's labor of love.

The big man was interested. He was also pleased with what he could see of the saddle. It was nearly finished, and Hugh assured him it would be ready in another week. Henning said he'd either come for it himself or send someone in from the ranch. He also said, "I heard Davy left a young buck with you as an apprentice who rode for him last season."

Hugh acknowledged that this was true. "Yep. George Jefferson."

Buster Henning's expression subtly changed as he said, "He's not here, is he?"

Hugh's surprise that an outlying cowman would know this would have been obvious if Henning had

52

been interested in altered expressions, which he wasn't. "No, he left day before yestiddy."

Henning began to roll a cigarette meticulously. With his eyes on what he was doing, he said, "Well now, Hugh, yesterday a couple of my riders was east a ways combin' along the foothills and heard what sounded like a gun duel back in the hills a ways, so they hid their horses and snuck up there."

Henning paused to fire up his quirley, trickled blue smoke in the direction of the new saddle, and continued. "It was that young apprentice of yours." Henning's steady gaze returned to Hugh's face. "One of my riders recognized him. They'd met a few times on the range."

Hugh's voice was sharp as he asked who had been out there with George, and Buster Henning said: "No one. He was settin' pine cones atop some rocks and shootin' them off. My boys watched for a spell then snuck back down and come home. Seems this apprentice of yours was practicing drawing and firing, an' they said it must not have been the first time he'd ever done this because he was almighty fast and dead accurate."

Hugh leaned on the counter while assimilating this bit of unexpected information. Buster Henning, a shrewd and perceptive individual behind his easygoing affability, waited a moment then asked if Hugh had any idea about why his apprentice was practicing with weapons. When Hugh shook his head the cowman gave him a rough slap on the shoulder and spoke as he was moving in the direction of the doorway. "We all did that when we was about his age. But when he comes in I'd take it kindly if you'd tell him I got cattle in those foothills, an' I don't like folks throwin' lead around up there."

53

Hugh was still leaning on the counter, staring off into space, when another visitor entered the store. Hugh looked around without enthusiasm until Joe Fogarty said, "Well, I got quite a story to tell you." Fogarty went past Hugh to lift the speckleware coffeepot off the stove and fill a cup before turning back toward the counter. "To begin with—where is George?"

Hugh made a vague gesture. "Out yonder somewhere."

Fogarty surprised Hugh with a resounding statement. "Good. That makes things easier." He took his cup to the counter, put it down, and looked steadily at the older man. "I hired a horse an' rode out northwest of San Luis to meet some hardscrabble stump-ranchers near where the lad was born an' raised." Joe paused to taste the coffee. "They spun me quite a tale. The marshal in town said they might. He didn't seem to want to talk much about the lad or his mother except to mention a couple of scrapes the lad got into up there an' to say his mother was a beautiful woman with a heart of gold and a quiet sadness that stuck out like a sore thumb.

"Those stump-ranchers had more to tell. Seems the lady was on hard time some years back when a cowman met her an' commenced takin' supplies out to her shack from the store in San Luis."

Hugh went to draw himself off a cup of java and returned behind the counter with it. He was beginning to have an inkling about something.

Fogarty went on speaking. "She come up pregnant."

Hugh nodded very slightly. "The lad's a catch colt?"

"Yes. She gave birth alone in her cabin."

"Who was his father?"

"They didn't know. They'd seen the cowman a number of times, but he wasn't from around the San

54

Luis country and since he never came back after George was born, they didn't make any effort to find out his name."

Hugh ran a callused thumbpad around the rim of thecoffee cup and remembered something Joe Fogarty knew nothing about: a tightfisted, self-centered, overbearing cowman coming down off his high horse and virtually begging Hugh to take in an apprentice. Even putting up a little pouch of money to sweeten the pot. In a quiet voice he said, "That son of a bitch."

Fogarty's eyed widened. "Who?"

"Whoever he was that got her into that fix then never went back."

Fogarty accepted that as a general statement. He had a little more to add to what he'd already said. "The lad grew up quick with his fists, fearless as a bitch-wolf, and troublesome after he was big enough to show it. He worked around up there, and no one ever said he wasn't conscientious an' real handy. An old In'ian who lived out there among those shack-folks told me he'd taught the lad to plait and braid. His judgment was that the lad was heading straight for an early grave.

"Then he got to working the ranches and eventually came down here lookin' for work."

Hugh nodded. "Barber said he was a top hand young as he was."

As though Pepperdine had not spoken, Joe Fogarty went on. "All the folks up there knew was that about six months or so after he'd left the country, his mother left, too. No one had any idea where she went—but we know, don't we?"

Hugh did not reply. He emptied his cup and set his back to the counter, eyeing the new saddle. "Somethin' you'd ought to know, Marshal. The night of the same

55

day you left to go up yonder, George snuck out in the middle of the night and hasn't come back. Buster Henning's riders saw him yesterday up in the foothills west of the grave, practicin' with a six-gun." Hugh turned to face the larger and younger man. "They said he was fast and dead accurate. James an' I was worried that he'd figured out some way where you'd gone an' was lookin' for you up there. I guess that was wrong. He went up into the hills to hone his skill with a six-gun."

Fogarty's brows dropped a notch. "For me?"

Hugh shook his head. "Naw, not for you. If he was fixin' to come after you for openin' that grave, he'd more'n likely have been waitin' up in the corralyard today."

Marshall Fogarty eyed the saddle- and harnessmaker for a long moment, finished his cup of coffee, and said, "You expect him to come back?"

Hugh nodded without looking away from the saddle, and after Joe Fogarty had departed he went back to work on the saddle, but slowly and thoughtfully. He was still working on it when McGregor came over because he'd seen Joe Fogarty leave Hugh's shop.

McGregor said, "I see Joe's back."

Hugh's smile was humorless. "Yeah. An' you're nosy."

McGregor bristled. "Don't I have a right to be?"

Hugh nodded. "Sure. Want some java?"

"No."

Hugh repeated almost word for word what the marshal had reported, and McGregor did finally go fill a cup at the stove, but he didn't drink from it. He leaned on the counter gazing pensively at his old friend. "I'd about half figured that was it. A catch colt. Nothin' was

56

ever said about his pappy. You want to know what else I figured?"

Hugh's reply was dry. "It's open season."

"Davy Barber's his paw."

Hugh neither conceded this nor denied it. He approached the counter to fish on a shelf below it for that bottle of malt liquor he'd belatedly hidden when Hank Dennis had been in. He set it atop the counter and nodded toward the untouched cup of coffee. "Give it some backbone if you want to."

McGregor didn't want to. "If he's practicin' with a gun, Hugh, it could mean he knows who got his maw pregnant then abandoned her."

Pepperdine shook his head. "Remember that note he wrote out an' buried with her? Well, my guess is that that's the question he was forever askin' her an' she wouldn't ever answer for him. Maybe because she knew he'd kill Davy an' maybe get hanged for it. I doubt that she cared much what happened to Davy, but from what Joe learnt up yonder, that boy was her whole life. She wouldn't want him to do somethin' that'd ruin him."

McGregor eyed the cup, unscrewed the cap off the whiskey bottle, and tipped his head. He blew out a breath, put the bottle aside, and said, "Where is the damned fool?"

Hugh was unshakable in his conviction about that. "He'll be along."

McGregor, with a less favorable outlook on life and those who lived it, said, "Yeah. So'll Christmas," and left the shop.

It was a warm afternoon, but for the first time in a long while there were huge cloud-galleons moving toward the Sheridan Plains from beyond the northeasterly mountains, and they had the soiled gray borders that presaged the nearing end of autumn and the approach of winter.

Storm clouds.

There was no air stirring; mane and tail hair splayed and remained that way on tethered horses along Main Street. Down at Reg Lee's combination livery and trading barn the paunchy proprietor was sweating like a stud horse in the middle of his perpetually gloomy runway exchanging morose grumblings with his swamper. The swamper was an old, scrawny, sinewy former Confederate soldier who once a month, as regular as clockwork, loaded up at Rusty's saloon, staggered back down to the lower end of town, and sank down upon his bedraggled assortment of discarded blankets, croaker sacks, and sweat-stiff saddle pads to sing in a cracked voice just two songs. One was Dixie, the other one was Lorena—maybe, when the grass was green again, they'd meet.

Obviously they hadn't.

The swamper was leaning on a manure fork in the middle of the runway as he said, "He don't overwork the horses, an' he pays on the barrelhead, but damned if I can figure where a harness shop apprentice gets any money. But this time I'm glad it was you let him have the horse, because if it was me an' he didn't return for three days, you'd be all over my carcass like a damned rash."

Reg mopped sweat. "Now that ain't so an' you know it. When did I ever get onto you for—?"

"The most recent time," the swamper said quickly, "was when I give Dr. Pohl that big Morgan mare on his buggy because his own horse had Monday-mornin' sickness."

"Well, I didn't know his damned horse was sick."

The old soldier's sunk-set eyes were sulphurous as he contemplated his employer. They got along like this quite well and had been doing it the same way for three years. "You could have asked why I give him the Morgan mare first before you come down on me like a ton of stone."

Reg continued to mop. "Damn, it's humid today."

"Storm's coming an' sure as hell winter's right behind it."

Reg shuffled up near the front of the barn where little breezes usually came along in the late afternoon; but not today, and the old Secesh was right. There were clouds moving with the inexorable and ponderous slowness of eternity. He watched them for a long time. It took a long time to determine that they were heading for the Sheridan country.

A man didn't have any more sense than a goose to stay in a place where winter lasted four months, snow lay thick for another month after that, and it got so cold a man had to use a crowbar to crack ice off water troughs.

The swamper called sharply from down near the back-alley end of the runway. Reg turned and shuffled down there with sweat running under his shirt in rivulets.

The old swamper pointed with a skinny arm. Whatever else he lacked, perfect eyesight was not one of them. "There he is, ridin' along on a loose rein like he didn't have a care in the world."

Reg had to shield his eyes, and even then he couldn't make out any of the details of the distant rider. "You sure it's him?"

The swamper lowered his arm and leaned on the manure fork again without answering the question.

"He'll owe you a dollar an' a half. Reg, that horse looks better'n when he rode out of here on him."

Lee was still squinting below his shading hand. But this time he wouldn't admit he couldn't see that far very well. "Yeah, an' for your information that's why I wasn't worried. He's never taken a horse out that he didn't bring it back lookin' good."

The old soldier put a pithy took on his employer. He did not speak, but his expression did: a man couldn't work around another man for three years without knowing that while his acquaintance, in this case his employer, could see the end of his nose with absolute fidelity, he couldn't see details of things he looked at across a damned road.

The swamper turned back to his work leaving Reg to collect what was owed for the rented horse.

Those enormous storm clouds continued their slow advance; the humidity, which had been increasing all day, continued to increase; and finally, about the time the solitary horseman entered the back alley heading for the rear of the barn, a few gusts of a cold wind whistled down through town.

Summer was past, autumn was yielding, the old Rebel was right; behind the oncoming storm was winter.

CHAPTER 8

Some Oncoming Clouds

HUGH HAD FINISHED WITH THE SEATING LEATHER AND was rolling it to force a wrinkle-free fit using one of those old pestles the country was littered with and that prehistoric squaws had used to grind, among other things, juniper berries and shriveled dry meat. He was distracted less by the slowly accumulating early gloom than he was by those directionless gusts of cold wind. When they persisted he put the round stone aside and strolled to the doorway to look at the sky. There were times when a man's nose was the best indicator of a change in the weather.

The immense wall of clouds was awesome. Hugh turned to reenter the shop and stopped dead in his tracks as George said, "It took a little longer'n I figured. You can fire me if you want to."

The lad did not look any different, but this time he had not removed the belt and weapon to hide them; he was wearing them.

Hugh scowled and jerked his head for George to follow him inside. The lad's expression was serene, almost indifferent, as Hugh said, "Who the hell said anythin' about firin' you, an' I'll tell you another thing, Mr. Henning wasn't too happy about you havin' target practice up where he's got cattle grazing around."

George looked steadily at Hugh, still expressionless. "There weren't no cattle. I made sure of that first."

Hugh hoisted one ham to the edge of the worktable while gazing at his apprentice. "George, I don't know what I'm goin' to do with you, but it'd sure make things a lot simpler if we could just talk man-to-man." He did not allow the youth any opportunity to reply. "There's somethin' else I can tell from livin' as long as I have: Right when a body thinks they got a secret is the exact time when they don't."

George tipped back his old hat and leaned on the counter, still expressionless, still mute. His gaze drifted to the new saddle, lingered briefly, then drifted back to Pepperdine.

Hugh had only begun. "Your maw was right, boy; leave it be, put it out of your mind, because more'n likely you're never goin' to get an answer."

The youth's eyes widened steadily as he regarded Pepperdine. "What are you talkin' about?" he asked very quietly.

Hugh took down a big breath. "Your paw."

"What about my paw?"

"Nothing. Absolutely nothing."

George slowly removed his old hat and just as slowly placed it on the counter. After a moment he raised his eyes to the older man's face again as he spoke. "Maybe you're right, maybe we'd ought to have a talk, an' you can start off by tellin' me what you know, which seems to be a hell of a lot for a feller that don't go a hunnert yards in any direction from this shop."

Hugh smiled. That was the longest continuous string of words that had come out his apprentice since they'd first hitched horses. He viewed it as a promising beginning, but he did not answer George's question. Instead, he set forth the ground rules for their palaver by saying, "When you was growin' up out west of San Luis, didn't you ever talk to the other folks out there?"

"Sure I talked to 'em. There was an old bronco who lived in a soddy with his old woman. He was my friend. There were others. What about it?"

"Your paw, boy."

George briefly hung fire. . . . "They didn't know. All they told me was that he rode good horses, sort of looked like ten thousand other fellers, an' when I asked around in town it was like talkin' to a bunch of trees."

Hugh nodded. "And what about your maw?"

George's jaw muscles rippled. "She'd smile and maybe brush my hair back or maybe find a stick of jerky to shove in my mouth. I kept at it. The last time was when she was sick up in her foothill camp."

Hugh nodded about that, too. "I got to hand it to you, son, you never give up. I mean—that note you scribbled an' buried with her."

George's gaze dropped to the old hat and remained there. "I had a right to know, Mr. Pepperdine."

Hugh had to dig for the right answer to that. "Maybe. Depends on why you wanted to know, George." As the younger man's gaze returned to his face, Hugh also said, "Practicin' with a gun don't convince me you want to know who he was so's you can go shake his hand."

The youth's eyes brightened and hardened. "I'm goin' to find out who he was, an' I'm goin' to kill him."

One of those bitter gusts of wind stirred dust in the roadway and rattled loose roof boards. Hugh waited until the noise passed before speaking again. "Light that lamp behind the stove while I light the other ones. We're in for a storm."

While they were working at this a clap of thunder struck somewhere north of town, but it might as well have been directly overhead because every window and half the doors in town violently quivered.

Hugh turned in time to see George wince. He acted as though he had not noticed as he reached for his hat and yelled above the gathering wind. "We better get down to the cafe and have supper before all hell busts loose. Come along."

Nature had provided them both with something they needed: a lengthy diversion to use in getting their thoughts together for the next time they talked.

Half the town evidently had arrived at the same conclusion Hugh had. The cafe was filling up by the time they got down there. While men waited for their suppers they discussed only one topic: the approaching storm.

It hadn't been an especially dry summer, except in the view of range stockmen, and no matter how often rains arrived during the grazing season, they always complained. But this storm was clearly not going to be a warm autumn downpour but rather the swan song of a departing season.

The cafeman was sweating despite those gusts of cold wind. When someone ribbed him about piling money into his cash drawer he snapped back, "You try this for a while and see how you like it!"

That dampened everyone's mood but did not have any effect on either the harnessmaker or his apprentice. They ate without a word passing between them, finished, paid up, and returned to the roadway just in time to see dust explode out where horse traffic had been grinding the soil to the consistency of flour for months.

Hugh reset his hat, paused long enough to skive off a chew with his clasp knife, pouch it into his cheek, and jerk his head as he struck out for the opposite duckboards. George hunched up against the fitful wind but there was nothing he could do about the raindrops that were beginning to become smaller in size and greater in volume.

By the time they reached the shop, waves of water were advancing against the town in close-spaced ranks. Hugh dug some pots from beneath the counter and went around placing them where leaks were beginning to show water—the same places he'd been placing receptacles for several years. When he straightened up, smiling ruefully, he yelled above the drumroll on the roof.

"You better check your ceiling. It leaks in there now and then, an' this is one of those 'then' times."

After George had departed Hugh went around adjusting lamp wicks to avoid excessive smoking, which not only smudged the ceiling but made glass mantles difficult to clean. It was a chore he did not like particularly.

When George returned he was shaking his head. "Comin' on a slant," he yelled, "makin' the window leak. I stuffed some rags around it."

"Mind checkin' my room?"

The youth turned away leaving Hugh over by the front window, looking out. Visibility was very limited even though the rain had scrubbed the outer segment of the window. There was just too much water to see beyond the plankwalk.

Hugh sighed and went back to see if there were embers in the stove. Fortunately there were. He shoved some kindling in, blew on the smoke until a fingerling of fire shot up, then closed the door, set the damper, and shook the coffeepot. It was heavy with grounds, not water. He got another fistful of ground beans and dropped them in, added some water, and went around to the working area to contemplate Buster Henning's saddle. He was unaware that George had come in from out back and was no longer wearing his shellbelt and six-gun until the lad came over beside him to eye the saddle. He said, "Mr. Pepperdine?"

"Yes."

"About my mother."

Hugh turned. "We'll have to wait until the storm lets up."

George nodded about that. "If I had a little advance on my wages, I could buy her a decent box."

George swallowed the lump in his throat. "Sure. As much as you want. The town carpenter's name is Harald Johnson, with an 'a' instead of an 'o.' He lives down behind the blacksmith's shop. He's usually got a few coffins leanin' out back." For a moment Hugh studied the tall youth's profile then reached and gave him a rough slap across the shoulders. "Just bear up, partner. In this damned life it's one blow after another. I used to try to figure out why. Then I just commenced to take 'em as they come. . . . I think that coffee's hot. You like a little panther juice in yours?"

The lad inclined his head without taking his eyes off the Henning saddle. When Hugh returned with two cups, one laced liberally, one barely laced at all, he gestured with the hand holding the cup. "Every time I make a saddle I wonder how much longer it'll last than I will. The first saddle I ever owned had been through the War of 1812, an' it was still as sound as the day it was made. This here one—maybe it'll still be in use a hunnert years from now." Hugh leaned to point. "Right there's where I put my name, the name of the town, an' the date." He straightened up, sampled the coffee, and smacked his lips. "A hunnert years from now won't a soul remember who Hugh Pepperdine of Sheridan was."

George went to the window to look out. He could see even less than Hugh'd been able to see because as the storm advanced against the town its force increased.

Hugh remained back by the saddle. He hadn't completed what he'd started out to say, which was simply that he didn't make saddles for men, he made them for horses.

A stagecoach came heavily into town from the south, broad, rear, steel tires sinking four inches at every rotation. Behind them water tumbled into the runnels and immediately began deepening them. The coach turned up into the corralyard and was no longer visible to people at windows on both sides of Main Street.

Hugh turned up the lamp nearest his working area, and placed the emptied coffee cup aside. As he went to work he yelled toward the front of the shop.

"George, you know what a running-W is?"

The youth turned. "No. Some kind of branding iron?"

"No. Take the junk out of that wooden box and set it out atop the worktable. I'll show you."

George did as he'd been told, except that when he removed everything from the box, he had no idea how to arrange any of it until Hugh walked over, speaking loudly as he placed the pieces where they belonged.

"Those hobbles are placed on a horse's front ankles. An' this used to be a ring-halter. See; this ring fits down where the curb strap would be on a bridle. An' this here is the surcingle. It goes around the horse's middle like in a drivin' harness. See those two rings on the side of the surcingle? Well, let's go back to the hobbles. A man ties a length of rope to the ring in each hobble. Or he can use twelve-foot leather wagon lines. Now then, he runs them lines up through the ring on the halter an' back through them smaller rings on the surcingle an' he's ready."

"For what?"

"To break a horse of the worst darned habit they get. Running away."

"How does it work?"

"You get everything buckled into place, then you get behind the horse with the lines in your hands like a farmer, then you slap his rump with the lines an' when he bolts you pay out leather, yell 'whoa' at the top of your lungs an' when he don't pay any attention to that, you set back with the lines, which yanks his ankles out from under him an' down he comes on his nose."

George was scowling. "Pretty rough treatment, Mr. Pepperdine."

Hugh smiled. "Yes sir it sure is. Now an' then a horse loses a front tooth, but not often. George, did you ever have a horse run away with you?"

"No. Just buck is all."

"There's no comparison. A buckin' horse runs down after a while or he dumps you an' heads for home leavin' you to walk home. A runaway horse'll kill a rider or folks in a buggy about half the time. A running-W's only purpose is to teach the horse that when someone yells whoa and sets back on the lines, he'd better pay attention or he's going to have one hell of a headache."

"You used them?"

Hugh nodded. "Many times."

"Do they really break a horse from runnin' away?"

"Nine times out of ten they do."

"What about the tenth time?"

Hugh wagged his head. "Lead the horse far back up in a canyon an' shoot him. If you don't, if you can't stop him from bolting, sooner or later he'll either kill you or someone else. Maybe a mother takin' her little girl for a buggy ride to see wildflowers in springtime. . . . Hey, water's comin' under the damned door!"

A deafening roll of thunder drowned out the last half of Hugh's final remark, and as he sprang ahead to stuff rags behind and under the roadway door, George moved just as quickly to help him.

CHAPTER 9

A Time to Remember

THIS WAS ONLY THE BEGINNING. RAIN COWED Sheridan and the countryside for three days. It washed ditches in the roadway a dog could get lost in. It battered roofs until half the buildings in town had soggy walls and floors, and the other half would have sagged on their fir-log foundations if brave souls hadn't put on rain hats and rubber ponchos to go out there and shovel diversion ditches like their lives depended upon it.

Morton's saloon had a stove going day and night for the bedraggled customers who made it over there. The cafeman did some business, too, mostly in scalding hot coffee and steaks.

At Dennis's store, while Hank and his elderly clerk with the black cotton sleeve protectors were working like slaves to prevent water that was over the plankwalk from coming under the roadway door, some chocolatey mud from the alley on the east side of town seeped in from out back, flooded the storeroom, and ruined several oak barrels of salted beef and flour.

Up at the corralyard Silas scuttled around under his huge hat wearing a shiny, black, rubber poncho that made him look like a pterodactyl without wings and croaked orders at his yardmen whose faces ran equal parts sweat and rainwater as they trenched water away from the feed sheds and the horse stalls. Nothing could be done for the yard itself, which was a quagmire.

Hugh and George were better off than many folks. They had leaks, had to empty pots every hour or two, and added to the sound of the fierce storm outside was the hissing of the iron stove where leaking water came down the stove pipe and hit the hot iron. But they at least had plenty of firewood under the eaves out back and food enough. They also had their work. Hugh left off working on Henning's saddle long enough to teach his apprentice how to make a new running-W.

There was also a small backlog of other work; so for most of the time the town was paralyzed by the storm, they worked with one eye on the ceiling, the other one on their work, and unconsciously listened for the diminution of the racket until, on the third day, it finally came.

With a cold drizzle falling Joe Fogarty came up to the shop stamping off mud and wagging his head as he said, "Damndest thing I ever saw. Lee's barn's got a gully down through the runway a man's got to leap across. Hank's storeroom is a shambles." Joe paused to look around at the pots on the floor, the dripping ceiling, the hissing stove, and the places where Hugh and his apprentice had been working. He said, "You must live right."

Hugh asked about McGregor, and Joe shrugged. "He went around with a chisel, a hammer, and some cloth calking the walls like his shop was a ship. He came through it pretty fair. Got some mud to shovel off the floor out front but otherwise all right." Joe eyed George Jefferson, who returned the look without wavering until Hugh broke up the eye duel by saying, "Any stages running?"

Fogarty swung his gaze back to Hugh. "No. Not even the mail coach. Silas said it'll be a week before the roads'll be fit to use."

On the fourth day the sun arrived, steam rose over the

70

entire countryside, and for once the loafers around town were courted by everyone who needed help digging out. Only Rusty Morton didn't have much trouble because his building was higher than the plankwalk. His business picked up, too, along toward the evening of the fourth day, which was about the time the winds arrived.

They usually did, so that surprised no one, but because walking was dangerous they frayed a lot of tempers that were not very good to start with.

It was too wet to use Fresno scrapers to fill in the roadway runnels until about the seventh day after the storm, and when Hugh rolled out on the eighth day he got a shock. Six inches of fluffy snow covered everything.

He fired up the stove while George brought in a couple armloads of wood. Hugh was exasperated. "It's not supposed to snow for another five, six weeks."

George's retort made Hugh eye him askance. George said, "Mother Nature don't have a calendar," and continued filling the wood box.

The snow fell lightly but steadily until there was over a foot on the flat, much more on the the sides of structures, and even more in the northward mountains; but at least people could make headway in snow, which they hadn't been able to do during the torrential downpour. One of the first people to enter the harness works after Hugh had shoveled snow away from out front was Silas Browning, no longer wearing the old bat-wing poncho but still wearing his oversized hat. And also bundled up in an old blankcoat two sizes too large.

Silas, like a lot of other people around town, was in a vile mood. When Hugh innocently asked if he'd been able to get a stage running, Silas glared. "In a foot of snow when a driver can't see the washouts? What kind of a damned fool question is that?"

Hugh let that pass as he went over where George had just about completed the running-W. "Couldn't do anything with the busted one, Silas, so we made you a new one."

Browning approached the counter as he sniffed and scowled. He picked up part of the rig, held it so light would reveal any uneven stitching or hints of neck or shoulder leather, and astonished Hugh by saying, "Now that's a good piece of work." Then, as though surprised at himself, he dropped it and shot Hugh a bleak look. "I never authorized you to make a new one. I said patch—"

"It couldn't be patched, Silas. I told you that. There's the box. You can take it with you. All them scraps is there." Hugh returned the old man's bleak look as he said, "George, hang it on the wall. Someone'll come along, a horsebreaker or maybe—"

"Wait a minute," Silas croaked as George was picking up the rig. "Boy, just leave it there. Hugh, I never told you to make it for me, but if you'll shave somethin' off that seven dollars, I'll take it."

The old man made his annoying sniffing sound, and Hugh's hackles rose. But with George watching them both, Hugh knew better than to explode. He smiled at Silas Browning. "Take it to the window where the light's better. Look it over real careful. It's got only back leather. Examine the sewing. Four strands twisted tight and waxed. Silas, that outfit will last longer'n you, me, and the lad here. . . . Six-and-a-half dollars an' that's it, you old screwt, take it or leave it."

Silas drew forth a long leather purse with a snap closure on its top. In order to get coins from the bottom of the thing he had to push upwards from the bottom. Hugh and George watched. It was almost a ritual the way Silas counted out each coin, and unbeknownst to either of the watchers, he put in a counterfeit two-bit piece he'd been carrying for six months for just such an occasion.

After Silas had departed carrying the new running-W, George shoved a piece of red fir into the stove, looked at Hugh, and burst out laughing.

Hugh did not join in. He was still boiling.

George said, "Look here."

"What is it?"

"A two-bit piece made of pure lead."

"Why, that connivin' old son of a bitch, I'm goin' up there and kick the wadding out of him."

Hank Dennis came stamping in. The sky was dark, and it was beginning to snow again. Hank's nearly bald scalp was covered by a woolen cap down to the ears. He was wearing a red-and-black Hudson's Bay blanket made into a coat and bearskin gloves. Before he said a word he backed up to the stove. He eyed Hugh speculatively for a moment, then spoke. "I got one hell of a mess down at the store. Back room's got four inches of mud on the floor." He paused to look away then back again. "You don't look like you suffered much."

Hugh agreed. "Some leaks is about all."

The storekeeper nodded, flicked a glance at George, then said, "I been tryin' to hire some of those saloon bums to help us clean up."

Hugh's eyes narrowed a notch. He knew what was coming, but he waited.

Hank cleared his throat. "I was thinkin' that if you didn't need your helper here for maybe the rest of the day . . . I'd pay him goin' wages and see that he'd be fed good."

Hugh looked at George. "It's up to you."

George considered the merchant. He knew who he was, but that was about all he knew. "I guess there's not much to do here for a spell, Mr. Pepperdine."

Hugh nodded, and as the pair of them were leaving the shop, he called after them. "Hank? How much does a coat like that cost?"

Dennis stopped and looked back. "Well, fifteen dollars is the goin' price. Pretty expensive, but—"

"Fifteen dollars for crissake," Hugh exclaimed. "That's more'n most men earn in a month."

"I know that, but this here is one hunnert percent wool from the Hudson's Bay Company. Down in the city they sell for up to thirty dollars, Hugh. But if you want one . . ."

"I was thinkin' of the lad, Hank. He don't own a decent winter coat."

"Well . . . Let me think about it."

Hugh smiled to himself as he watched them gingerly cross through deep snow to the far plankwalk and struggle southward. Silas wasn't the only one who could be a devious old scoundrel when the occasion arose.

He stoked the stove so the shop would remain warm during his absence and forced his way through deep snow to McGregor's shop. Some humanitarian had poked red sticks in the roadway where the deepest erosion gullies were, which prevented some nasty falls and maybe even some broken ankles or legs.

James was wearing mittens from which the upper half of the fingers had been cut away. He'd made a fresh pot of coffee, which he shared with Pepperdine as they talked about the weather. McGregor was of the opinion

74

that fall winter had arrived early, was going to continue bad, and would not let up until late next spring.

When Hugh challenged this prediction McGregor waved airily in the direction of the northward mountains. "Didn't you see the wisps of smoke up there?"

"No. What wisps of smoke?"

"Way back, deep in the mountains where the holdouts and reservation-jumpers got their secret rancherias. They've been makin' meat up there for a month now, I've never known it to fail, Hugh. When In'ians make meat early we're goin' to have a real bad winter."

Hugh was highly skeptical but kept that to himself. He remarked about Hank Dennis coming along to hire George to help swamp out the general store and recounted the episode about Silas and the lead two-bit piece.

James almost smiled. "You'd ought to have known he'd try somethin' like that. Silas's just plain got to believe he's skinned somebody. He's done things like that to every merchant in town. I'm surprised he hasn't tried it on you before."

"He has," stated Pepperdine. "That's why I set the price of that running-W at seven dollars. The goin' price is four dollars."

"If he ever finds out he'll go around town screamin' like a wounded eagle. You care for a little whiskey in the java?"

Hugh held out his cup. After both cups had been laced McGregor looked out at the steadily falling snow. He said, "You ever get the feelin' it'll never stop snowing?"

Hugh shrugged. "It's done me a good turn. It an' that damned rainstorm."

He smiled at the gunsmith. "The lad come out of his shell. When he found that lead two-bit piece in the money Silas left on the counter, he laughed. James, he's been in the shop since last fall, an' that's the first time I ever heard him laugh." Hugh winked at McGregor. "He comes right out and talks now, too. An' you know what else? Now an' then we get to rehashing a few things."

McGregor held his exposed fingers above the popping little, elegant-legged potbelly stove. "We'd better get his mother buried. I know; Harald told me he sold the lad a coffin at half price, and Henry Pohl said they nailed her into it an' put her out back in Hank's icehouse, but the sooner she's put down the better."

Hugh understood all this, but the weather hadn't permitted a burial, and from the looks of things right now, it might be a while before such a thing was possible.

McGregor had a question: "Does he say anythin' about his paw?"

"No. Not lately. Not since just before the first storm hit."

"Well, unless I got him figured all wrong, it's there; it's inside him."

Hugh finished the coffee, shot a look out where drifts were building up, and shrugged. "I know. But for the time bein' it might be in our favor that there's nothin' he can do but the same thing the rest of us are doing: Keep warm, don't burn so much wood we run out, an' wait for spring."

Hugh changed the subject by pointing to a pile of silver waiting to be buffed. "You gettin' stocked up?"

"Nothin' else to do. Might as well have a big display handy when summer rolls around and the cowboys come back."

Hugh left the shop, stood under its leaky old warped overhang studying the fishbelly sky, and threw a glance southward down toward the lower end of town. As far as falling snow permitted, he could see no signs of life, but the fragrance of wood smoke was in the air, as it had been for a month now and probably would continue to be for another two or three months, unless James was right, in which case folks would be keeping their stoves fired up until late into the summer; but Hugh doubted that.

He'd seen more than his share of bad winters, and to those like James who gloomily predicted the worst, whether it was snowing or the sun was boiling hot, he had always believed as he'd once heard an old man say when he'd been young. When someone was groaning about a drought and saying that all the crops would shrivel and the ground crack bone-dry, the old man had said, "It'll rain." When he'd been pressed, he'd also said, "It always has, hasn't it?"

This winter among winters would end. Winters always had ended, hadn't they?

CHAPTER 10

The Return of Spring

IT TURNED OUT TO BE ONE OF THOSE BETWIXT AND between situations. The winter did eventually end, but as McGregor had predicted, it did not depart fully until late into the following spring.

Sheridan resounded to hammers, profanity, and horses snorting under strain as Main Street was filled, tamped and leveled, roofs were repaired, a few log foundations were jacked up high enough for big, flat stones to be inserted beneath them, and Hank Dennis did a thriving business peddling nails and whatnot even before the cowmen returned as the grass went from watery pale green to good, hard, dark green.

George had put on a little lard, which Hugh, Marshal Fogarty, James McGregor, and a few other folks around town who'd come to know him during the bad winter kept reminding him about.

The first time in months that Hugh saw the darkly brooding look return to George's face was when they buried his mother in the cemetery a half mile northeast of town on some raised ground that had a little iron fence around it.

He also noticed something else; about half the town had turned out with Sunday-go-to-meeting attire and scrubbed hands and faces. It pleased Hugh and McGregor, who stood together throughout the ceremony, that George had settled in so well.

McGregor made a little grumpy sound that Hugh ignored, so James dug him in the ribs with a bony elbow and jutted his jaw. With one of those traveling preachers intoning endlessly about the virtue of someone he'd never seen in life and knew nothing about, Hugh followed out the line of his friend's gesture.

George was standing slightly stooped. He was as tall as just about anyone out there. He had greased his boots, cuffed his old hat until it looked almost respectable, and was wearing a genuine Hudson's Bay blanket coat over a new white shirt. But what James had grumped about, and what Hugh noticed finally, was that Charlotte Dennis, Hank's very pretty, robust daughter, was standing so close to Hugh's apprentice that their hands and arms touched.

On the walk back to town James said, "How old's the lad now?"

Hugh based his reply on what Davy Barber had told him last year. "Nineteen."

James rolled that around in his head until they were almost back to Main Street. "Well, I was a year younger when I got married, an' my wife was sixteen."

Hugh frowned but said nothing. However, by the time he was in his back room, shedding his tie, coat, and burial-and-wedding pants, and climbing back into his everyday clothing, he remembered something that had happened last Christmas, and which up until now he'd thought of as simply a gesture of gratitude on Hank Dennis's part: the gift of that expensive blanket coat.

As he went out front to tie on his apron and give the completed Buster Henning saddle a quick rubbing with a piece of rough cloth, it also occurred to him that George had been leaving the shop every now and then after dusk; when they were at work the mornings after those outings, he seemed to have reverted to those earlier periods of preoccupied silence.

It was McGregor who finally put these things into perspective by telling Pepperdine that the only folks who were too blind to see were those who had never gone sparking seriously or who had never been married.

Hugh had mulled that over. His feelings were mixed and troubled, but he kept those things to himself. One day Buster Henning, even fatter in the spring than he'd been in the fall, drove into town with one of his riders. While the rider was over at the emporium so that Hank could begin loading supplies from the list the rider handed him, Buster entered the harness shop, where his finished saddle had been sitting since last winter, and beamed a wide smile at Hugh as he said, "That's a real

79

beauty, Hugh, an' just in time for the workin' season."

Hugh took the cowman around behind the counter and gestured. "Try it." The reason he'd said this was that, while most men put weight on in front, Buster had done it the way beavers—and women—did it: in the tail.

But the sixteen-inch seat was adequate. Buster was as pleased as a kid with a bag of new marbles. He counted out the money, tossed in an extra little bit as he said, "For the kid," and got himself a cup of java from the stove. While he was occupied doing this he inadvertently dropped a bombshell that scattered all of Hugh's other thoughts.

"Davy's wagon came up yesterday. The feller settin' up camp said the drive with the other hands'll be showin' up soon. Maybe within the next couple of days."

After Henning had left with the new saddle over one shoulder, still grinning from ear to ear as he headed toward the wagon in front of the general store, Hugh returned to work on a set of canvas housings for chain traces he'd been hired to do by Silas Browning.

George came in from out back with an armload of wood, saw the empty saddle rack, dumped the wood, and said, "It don't look right without the saddle, does it?"

Hugh agreed about that. "Nope. Not after it was around for so long." He smiled. "Ready to try your hand on one?"

"A saddle?" George exclaimed.

"Yeah. I'll lead you along. It's a good idea to have one handy what with the cattlemen gettin' things under way again." Hugh stopped sewing the tug cover. "Somethin' you might want to remember, George.

80

When a man works for himself he can loaf or he can commence to lay up an inventory. If he keeps workin', he'll eventually get paid for his time; if he loafs, he won't. And if you work for yourself what you're really doin' is selling your life in little pieces; hour at a time, day at a time, week at a time. An' since you don't have a life that's goin' to last forever, you got to work an' lay by."

The tall youth, who had filled out and come to look and act more mature this last year, nodded as though he either understood or had already been thinking along those lines himself.

Hugh got a knot in his stomach. Because George hadn't acted either surprised or particularly impressed about what Hugh had just explained to him, he would have bet a new saddle the youth had heard pretty much the same thing somewhere else.

Hank Dennis!

That evening Hugh was sitting alone in the shop when Marshal Fogarty walked in smoking a long, thin panatela cigar. Someone must have given it to him because to Hugh's knowledge he never bought cigars himself. He said, "I just heard somethin' interesting over at the saloon."

Hugh nodded. "Barber's coming."

Fogarty removed the cigar. "Yeah." He considered the grey ash. "Not counting the lad, there's only you'n me, McGregor, and Henry Pohl who know the lad's more'n likely Davy Barber's catch colt."

Hugh got a cud tucked into his cheek while he waited for the rest of it. It was a short wait.

"And—one other."

Hugh nodded about that, too. "Barber."

"Seems likely."

Hugh was remembering the last time he and the cowman had talked. Right here in his shop. "More'n just likely, Joe. He knows. How he knows I got no idea. Any more'n I got any idea how you knew the woman's first name was Helen."

Fogarty continued to study the ash on his stogie. "You never went up there, did you? Her name was scratched on a rock set in the ground as a headstone: Helen Jefferson." Fogarty returned the cigar to his mouth and shoved big hands deep into trouser pockets. "Did the lad ever mention his mother goin' down from her camp, maybe down on Barber's range or anythin' like that?"

"No. I'd remember if he had."

"Well, then, I think he and Davy must have got to talking. You know, when men ride out all day, maybe days at a time, they get to talking, and since this was uppermost in George's mind, eatin' away at him, eventually he'd talk about it."

Hugh shifted his cud while speculating that this was very probable. But these were not important issues to Hugh Pepperdine, so he brushed them aside when he said, "Like I told George, when folks think they got a secret is exactly when they don't have. You, James, Henry, an' I got this figured out, an' George filled in the parts we didn't know. And Davy knows. That's five people who know a secret about the lad that'll get someone killed sure as hell if it leaks out."

Marshal Fogarty blew fragrant smoke and leaned on the counter, studying the older man's face. "It won't leak out. Not from us here in town. Tell me something. Was George in the shop when Barber made you that proposition about takin' the lad on as an apprentice?"

"No. Davy had him stay outside with the wagon. But

there was somethin' else. Davy put up a lot of money to get me to keep the boy. He actually begged me, and that's worried me a little since then. If he was that concerned about George, who can say what it'll be like if they ever meet alone when Davy's been drinkin' or when he's made up his mind to tell the lad he's his father?"

Fogarty looked for a spittoon to drop his cigar into before replying. "Hugh, Davy's no fool. If George told him his story the way he feels about it, even a deaf man would be able to hear hatred in his voice."

Hugh thought that was probably correct. At least he wanted to think that it was. "All the same, I wish Davy'd take his cattle somewhere else."

Fogarty did not even comment on that because it clearly was not going to happen. He asked where George was this evening and got a shrug. "I didn't ask where he was goin', and he didn't tell me. But if you want a guess, I'd say he's wherever Hank Dennis' daughter is."

That did not appear to surprise Marshal Fogarty at all. In fact, he nodded his head about it. "That's maybe the best thing that's happened to him, except you, since he arrived in town. She's as sweet as they come. An' it's springtime Hugh, the sap is running."

As the marshal turned to leave he had one more comment to make. "I been turning somethin' over in my mind. That's why I came up here this evening. If I went out to Davy's camp took him aside and told him what I know, and told him if he ever breathes a word about it I'll break half the bones in his carcass, it might make him think a little."

Hugh slowly wagged his head. "It wouldn't scare him. He don't scare worth a damn, an' it just might

83

upset everything. Joe, it's not just the mess itself that worries me; it's the word getting around that George is a catch colt. If folks knew that he couldn't stay here one damned day after the gossip started." Hugh went over behind his counter to grope for the whiskey bottle, which he set in front of the larger and younger man. "He's come along better'n a green colt. He likes the shop, the town, he's made friends here—not countin' Charlotte Dennis—and if he can just put all that other crap behind him, he's got a good chance of really settlin' in and belonging."

Fogarty accepted the drink, lingered a little longer, then departed. Hugh had to light a couple of lamps to keep nightfall at bay. He had a couple of jolts himself before capping the bottle and shoving it back out of sight below the counter.

Across the road someone was hammering away again at Rusty's piano. If it had ever been tuned it must have been a long time ago, because every other chord sounded like a pair of wildcats fighting inside a croaker sack.

CHAPTER 11

Out!

WINTER WAS A MEMORY TO BE RESURRECTED occasionally, mostly among those who were not in business. For merchants the winter was one of those things like the croup or unsettling political situations that came and went.

Sheridan's economy gradually picked up as cattlemen resumed their normal, somewhat nomadic existence, while others, including ranchers, brought wagons to town to be repaired, or heaped with supplies for the working season ahead. The two most notable harbingers of good weather ahead, itinerant cowhands seeking work and a steady flow of stage-line passengers in town, pulled Sheridan out of its wintertime insularity.

Marshal Fogarty got his baptism the second week in May when three of Buster Henning's seasonal riders hoorawed the town on a Saturday night, and Rusty sent someone scuttling for the law.

Providing the cowboys were drunk, these events ordinarily amounted to more smoke than fire. This time only one of them was drunk, and the other two had taken on just enough of a load to feel ten feet tall and bulletproof.

When Joe entered the saloon a dead silence settled. The place was crowded, patrons about equally divided between rangemen and townsmen with a few travelers thrown in, but the travelers were already distancing themselves from what they deemed a local problem. They were in Sheridan to spend the night and to resume their travels the next morning.

Fogarty had a sawed-off shotgun in his hands when he entered the saloon, which was a time-honored way to get everyone's immediate attention.

The three rangemen had the bar all to themselves. Rusty's backbar had some shattered glass, some spilled whiskey, and a pale-faced proprietor back there beginning to edge clear the moment Marshal Fogarty came into the doorway with his big-bored shotgun held belly-high in both hands.

One of the cowboys was already beginning to wilt. Within moments he would dissolve into a heap on the floor, but before that happened one of his companions, a

85

rawboned, big-nosed man with pale blue eyes and lanky strength turned to eye the big man in the doorway with the shotgun. He made a half-growling laugh as he wagged his head. "Jake," he said to the man beside him, "look there. It's the army. Hey, Constable, what d'you figure to do with that blunderbuss?"

Fogarty gave an order. "Drop your guns. Both of you."

The other tall man, who was skinny with a very prominent Adam's apple that bobbled as he looked wide-eyed at the twin black holes aimed in his direction, spoke in a squeaky voice. "No call for that, Constable. We was just havin' a little fun."

Joe's gaze was fixed on the rawboned man whose expression was both defiant and contemptuous. "Drop it or I'll drop you!"

A patron over among the card tables on the north side of the room quietly spoke. "You better do it, cowboy."

The lanky man leaned back against the bar, hooked both thumbs in his shellbelt, and continued to sneer. "You ain't goin' to shoot anybody, Constable."

The explosion would have been loud in the roadway; inside the saloon it made ears ring for ten minutes after the last echo had died.

Both cowboys had jumped. The man with the Adam's apple caught his feet in the inert body of his friend on the floor. He went over backwards, pinwheeling with both hands and squawking. He made no immediate attempt to stand up.

His friend was no longer sneering. His face was red. He'd been made to look ridiculous by springing into the air when one of those two shotgun barrels had blasted. He made the ultimate mistake of twisting from the waist to mask the fact that he was going for his six-gun.

At a distance of no more than the width of the room Joe Fogarty's second blast lifted the cowboy into the air, carried him over the bartop, and dumped him behind it almost cut completely in two.

Ears still ringing from the earlier blast were completely deafened by the second one. Rusty Morton was standing up at the north end of his bar, getting whiter by the minute. The sight that had his insides churning was gratefully hidden from everyone else.

Rusty also had a big, ragged hole in the front of his bar, but at this moment he wasn't even sure where he was, let alone knew that Fogarty's first warning shot had ruined some of his woodwork.

The marshal hoisted the remaining cowboys to their feet, disarmed them, and made the man with the big Adam's apple carry his passed-out friend out into the night and down to the jailhouse.

It ruined the evening for Rusty's customers, who drifted away one and two at a time. It also ruined Rusty's evening. He covered the ground meat behind his bar with an old blanket, locked his front doors, and went to bed.

The following afternoon Buster Henning arrived in town riding on his new saddle, which was cinched to a twelve-hundred-pound horse whose only redeeming factor was that he could carry all that lard without difficulty.

Fogarty had fed his two prisoners, both of whom had the granddaddy of all headaches, tongues that resembled small, fur-bearing animals and expressions on their stubbly faces of men who simply could not believe what had happened.

Joe had recently returned from visiting Dr. Pohl and the town coffinmaker when Henning walked in and nodded. Fogarty nodded back, waved the big man to a chair, and said, "I warned him twice, Buster."

Henning nodded his head. "I know. I heard about it before I left the ranch. Well, I'll pay for the doctor to put him down an' for the box and all. How about the other two?"

Joe looked in the direction of the steel-reinforced, oaken cellroom door. "You can have 'em."

"No charge, no fine?"

"No. They looked pretty sick when I took some coffee and stew down to them an hour or so ago. Are they your permanent men?"

"No. Seasonal riders, but not here, not for me anyway. As soon as we get back to the ranch I'm goin' to pay them off. Sorry about this mess, Joe."

So was Joe, so was everyone else, but by the time Henning and his two sallow-looking rangemen were leaving town it was already beginning to be said that since something like this was bound to happen, and usually did only later in the season, maybe the irresponsible sons of bitches who flocked in to hire on would walk a little soft in Sheridan after this.

That was pretty much Hugh Pepperdine's feeling as he and George watched the new saddle go north past the shop. But Hugh pushed his judgment a little farther. As he was turning back to those canvas tug covers he said, "Every blessed summer, as far back as I can remember, it's been open season one way or another."

The burgeoning local economy touched every segment of communal existence to some degree, including the saddle-and-harness works. For about five weeks Hugh and George were too busy to return to subjects that last winter had occupied a good bit of their attention.

Just one thing remained constant; in fact became more visible. It had to do with George's nearly nightly visits to the Dennis house.

Hugh had become not only accustomed to this, he had belatedly become favorable about it. He'd never had more of a hold over the lad than had been specified from the beginning. He'd taught George a lot. There was still more to learn, but by the time the entire community knew Hank Dennis' girl and Hugh Pepperdine's apprentice were at the hand-holding stage, he'd told himself that maybe the saddle-and-harness business wouldn't be the youth's future. If things worked out between George and Charlotte Dennis, sure as hell Hank would want the lad to come into the emporium with him. And Hugh liked that idea, too. As he told James McGregor one night at the saloon, "There's more money in general storing in a month than there is in my shop all year."

McGregor nodded his acceptance of the drift of things. "She's a mighty fine young lady. Pretty as a yellow pony and smart . . . for a female."

That other thing was never far below Hugh's thoughts when George came up in a conversation, and McGregor was one of only two or three people he could talk to about it. "If nothin' comes along to wreck everythin' and ruin his life."

McGregor had evidently also been dwelling on this, because his reply was succinct. "I expect we could make certain it don't."

Hugh eyed the craggy-faced gunsmith but did not pursue this topic. A few days later he didn't even remember it, because as he was cleaning up alone before locking up for the night, Davy Barber walked in.

He didn't look or act any different then he had last

year, so maybe that talk about him having gotten married wasn't true. He still needed a haircut, a shave, and some clean clothing. His little eyes smiled as Hugh straightened up after removing his apron. He said, "Where's the lad?"

Hugh hung the apron up with his back to the cowman before replying. "Around town somewhere."

"How did he work out?"

Hugh crossed to the counter to lean there, eyeing the stockman. "Like you said, he learns fast, an' he's got real skill with his hands."

Davy looked around. "Business doin' well, is it?"

"Real well."

"Well now, you don't suppose the lad's been valuable enough for the last months to have commenced to earn his wages, do you?"

Hugh's jaw muscles rippled. "I'd say he has."

"Well, then, maybe I didn't have to give you all that money."

Hugh's anger stirred. He regarded the man he had less reason to tolerate this season than he'd had last season. "What are you aimin' at, Mr. Barber?"

"I was thinkin' that you could refund part of what I gave you."

Hugh continued to lean as he looked down at his work-roughened hands. It wasn't just the welching that increased his disgust; it was that Davy Barber clearly was going to distance himself from the obligation that had motivated him last year. He was going to abandon the boy exactly as he'd abandoned the boy's mother.

While Barber waited for Pepperdine to speak, he glanced out the window in the direction of the saloon. "They tell me there was a killin' over there last week."

Hugh's head came up slowly. "There's likely to be

one in here, too, if you don't leave."

Barber's head snapped around; his slatey eyes did not widen, they settled upon the harnessmaker's face and remained there. He obviously did not require an explanation. "I only done that out of the goodness of my heart, him being a waif an' all. Seems fair to me that if he learnt the trade and has been payin' his way—"

"*Out!*"

Hugh straightened up off the counter and was beginning to turn toward the end of it when the cowman said, "What the hell's wrong with you? I just made a suggestion. If you don't want to act fair an' give back some of the money, why then you can keep it." He went as far as the doorway and paused to add a little more. "You're gettin' awful cranky in your old age, an' you better watch that."

Hugh stalked to the empty doorway with fisted hands and watched the cowman cross over to where several rangemen were loafing at the tie rack in front of the saloon. He stopped among them and talked for a couple of minutes, then led the riders into the saloon. One of them, a graying, badly weathered man, stopped just before passing into the saloon and looked over in the direction of the harness shop.

Hugh went back to dig out that bottle under the counter and have a drink. That contemptible son of a bitch; Hugh shouldn't have said anything, he should have walked around to the front of the counter and hit Barber as hard as he could.

The following morning George brought two cups of coffee from the stove around to the working area, and as Hugh smiled his thanks and took the cup, George said something he'd been rehearsing since last night.

"Mr. Pepperdine, do you know Hank Dennis'

91

daughter?"

Hugh put the cup down slowly. This was the first time the subject had ever surfaced between them. He nodded his head. "Can't say as I know her, George, but I know who she is an' I've seen her around town since she was in pigtails."

"We're keepin' company."

Hugh nodded about that, too. "So I've heard. They tell me she's a real nice young woman."

"An' I want to ask her to marry me."

Hugh reached for the cup, but the coffee was too hot so he put it down again. "I never been married, but James has an' he told me he was younger'n you are when he got hitched double. What's she say about it?"

"I haven't asked her. I figured I should talk to you first."

Hugh's eyes lingered on the tall, muscular lad who had become a man right under his nose. "Son, she's the one you'd ought to talk to. Me, I just taught you a trade."

"Mr. Pepperdine, we been real close. I told Charlotte you'd have been my paw if I'd had anythin' to say about it. I told her I owed you a lot."

Hugh had to clear his throat before speaking again. "George, if I'd had a son I'd have been proud if you was him. Well; I want you to know I'm real happy for both of you, but you really ought to go talk to her."

"Right now, durin' workin' hours?"

George smiled. "Yep. Right now durin' workin' hours, because work will always be around, but gettin' married don't happen but once in a man's life. Mostly, anyway. Besides, there's nothin' here that won't wait. . . George, does her paw know?"

"I haven't spoken to him, but I think he's figured it

out."

Hugh nodded. The lad was right. Hank was shrewd; nothing likely to affect his only child would escape his notice. In fact, Hugh told himself, by now Hank had probably figured everything right down to tying the knot.

George shuffled his feet. Hugh reached for the cup again as he said, "Go, son. Hit while the iron's hot." At the tall youth's troubled look Hugh laughed. "Isn't any way to do somethin' like this except to grab the bull by the horns. Go on; standin' around here lookin' like sick as a tanyard pup isn't goin' to help. Go on."

George got untracked. He didn't even look back as he walked out into the sunlight and resolutely marched toward the opposite plankwalk.

Hugh sipped the coffee, grimaced, got the bottle, tipped in a decent amount of lacing, and took the cup with him back to the worktable.

An hour or so later Silas Browning, half-hidden beneath his oversized hat, walked in carrying several sets of driving lines. As he grunted them up onto the counter he said, "Thread wore out, Hugh."

Pepperdine looked at the lines. He hadn't made them, thank gawd. "Next time you buy drivin' lines, Silas, don't get 'em at some damned auction."

Browning took the rebuke well. He sniffed but that was all. "How soon can I have 'em?"

Hugh speared the old man with a testy gaze and waved his hand. "All this other work is ahead of you. Maybe next week."

Browning made his sound of sniffing annoyance again. "Can't send out stages without drivin' lines, Hugh."

Pepperdine's mood wasn't up to arguing, so he

nodded his head. "Day after tomorrow."

"All right. Where's the lad?"

"He's not here."

"You'd ought to keep that lad, Hugh. He's the best awl-an'-thread man I ever saw. He's even better'n you, an' you do a good job."

Hugh considered Silas for a long time then, approached the bar, dug out his whiskey bottle, and set it down, hard, on the counter.

Silas fled, muttering sizzling imprecations as he departed. Hugh smiled, put the bottle back beneath the shelf, and returned to work.

The morning, which had been clear and still, had yielded to an afternoon that was pleasantly warm, windless, and faintly fragrant. Hugh finished a couple of minor jobs and went to the roadside window to look down in the direction of the general store.

As usual there was a lot of movement down there, but there was no sign of George. For that matter there was no sign of Hank either. Just before he turned back toward the work area a dusty stagecoach—at least it was called that, but actually it was a mud wagon—entered town from the south with the driver hauling his hitch down to a walk. There was a town ordinance forbidding drivers of vehicles from letting their animals pass along Main Street at any other gait than a walk.

As the old rig passed, Hugh noticed its faded paint, its scars, and other signs of long usage. Stingy old Silas cared for the running gear and damned little else.

A graying woman was looking out of the rig on Hugh's side. He saw her face for moments before the coach passed along toward the corralyard. He'd never seen her before. At least, if he had, he didn't remember it as he went back to work.

94

CHAPTER 12

Another Season

HANK DENNIS LEFT HIS STORE AT THE PEAK OF THE morning trade and crossed over to the harness shop. He had a paper sack of Hugh's favorite chewing tobacco, which he placed atop the counter as he said, "No charge. We had to make room for a new box, and this was what was left in the old one."

Hugh expressed his gratitude, put the paper sack out of sight below the counter, and amiably said, "Busiest time of the day over yonder, isn't it, Hank?"

Dennis did not offer a denial. In fact, he did not reply to the question at all. He said, "Hugh, George asked Charlotte to marry him."

Pepperdine nodded and waited. Dennis was one of those rotund, very capable human beings who functioned largely on nerves, and when Hank was nervous he fidgeted as he was doing now. Hugh could have made it easier for Dennis, but he didn't. He was ninety percent sure he knew why Hank had come over. Because something was bothering him that was even more important than business: George Jefferson and his daughter.

Hank considered the serene expression of the larger man. He was picking his words carefully. "I know the lad's been your apprentice, an' I know he's not only a good worker an' honest an' all, but I know how it is when a person gets a good hired hand; he gets to depend on 'em."

Hugh finally relented. "Is there something wrong about him asking her?"

"Well—no."

Hugh's gentle look deepened. "Well, then, did she accept?"

". . . Yes. But—"

"Aren't no 'buts,' Hank."

"Hugh, I like the lad. He's decent and all, but I'm a father, an' the way a father looks at some feller who wants to marry his daughter is different from how his daughter looks at it. You understand that?"

Hugh nodded.

"I came over to ask you straight out about a couple of things I've heard about the lad."

Hugh's smile faded. "Such as?"

"For one thing, Buster Henning's rangeboss told me he saw George up in the foothills practicing with a six-gun. Practicin' drawing and firing."

Hugh spread big hands atop the counter. "Hank, maybe you never did that, but I sure as hell did, an' I expect nine-tenths of the fellers George's age have done it, too. It goes with growin' up. If you're worryin' about the lad bein' a gunman or anything like that, forget it."

Dennis seemed marginally reassured. "You'd know, I guess. You know him better'n anyone else."

"What else is botherin' you, Hank?"

"Well; he told Charlotte about his mother . . . .."

Hugh's shrewd eyes remained fixed on the merchant. "Your girl was out there when they buried her."

"Yes. Who was she, Hugh? Who is his father?"

This, of course, would have come up sooner or later. Hugh was not completely unprepared and gave the answer he'd decided to give. "If he told your girl about his mother then most likely he also told her he don't know who his father was."

Dennis bobbed his head up and down and shifted his

96

stance a little, shuffling his feet as he did this, and said, "You're close to him. Do you know who his father was?"

Hugh never batted an eye. "Nope, an' I wouldn't ask a man somethin' like that. Hank, you like the lad?"

"Yes. I told you I like him."

"An' he's honest, works hard, is careful with his money, an' don't have any bad habits. Nice lookin' boy. He'll take good care of your girl. Now tell me something: What the hell does it matter who his paw or grandpaw was, or anyone else in his family for that matter?"

"Charlotte's mother—"

"Hank, for crissake are you head of the family or is she? I'll tell you what I think, partner. I think if you or your missus start throwin' up obstacles, some mornin' the pair of you is goin' to wake up to an empty house. Young love don't put up with a lot of artificial obstacles. Your girl and the lad'll get a-horseback and the next time you'll see them—if your ever do—you'll be a lot grayer than you are now an' your missus will have balled up a ton of teary handkerchieves."

Hank Dennis paled and shifted his eyes to the back wall with its tin patterns then back to the countertop. They stayed there so long without Dennis saying a word that Hugh reached for the bottle under the counter, unscrewed it, and placed it directly in front of the merchant, then said, "Drink!"

Hank swallowed twice. He was not much of a drinking man, so water sprang into his eyes and for a moment his breath came in wheezy little gasps.

Hugh recapped the bottle and stowed it on the undercounter shelf as he gave a wintery smile. "You'n me have lived a' spell, Hank. We've seen a fair bit of

97

life. Now, maybe you've noticed this an' maybe you haven't, but I sure as hell have: Folks are born into trouble and go through life with it, an' you know what I figured out years ago? Two-thirds of it is unnecessary trouble; folks bring it on themselves. They worry it into existence." Hugh held up a hand because Dennis had opened his mouth to speak. "I don't know your girl real well but I sure as hell know the lad, an' I'll bet my life no matter how wonderful she is, she'll never in this damned world do any better." Hugh leaned on the counter. "This much I know about his mother. She loved him an' worried about him. She was a good mother and a fine woman. About his father . . . Who the hell cares?"

Dennis' color had improved over the last few minutes. He leaned, gave Hugh a rough slap on the shoulder, faced the doorway, squared his shoulders, and marched resolutely toward the roadway. As he passed the door he turned, nodded to the grizzled man standing there, and kept on walking.

McGregor eased around the doorjamb, and when Pepperdine saw him, James dryly said, "You ever consider the pulpit?"

Hugh studied his approaching old friend and began to redden. "You was listenin' just outside the door, you damned old haggis eater."

James shook the coffeepot, found it nearly empty, and placed it back atop the stove wearing a guileless expression. Even the insult did not dent his air of placidity. Nor did he deny having eavesdropped. He simply said, "You put it to him fair an' square. I'm proud of you. You still got that bottle under the counter?"

Hugh grudgingly leaned to feel for it and put it atop

the counter.

As the gunsmith removed the cap and raised the bottle he smiled. It was such a rarity that Hugh stared. After a couple of swallows, McGregor shoved the bottle toward the harnessmaker. "It came to me while I was listenin' that it's a damned good thing you didn't get the religious infection when you was younger or you'd have been another screamin' preacher like old John Brown."

Hugh took one swallow and put the bottle away as he said, "You know Hank's wife? I've never had reason to more'n nod to her."

The gunsmith did indeed know Hank Dennis's wife. "I helped make the scaffolding when they wanted to paint the church some years back. She was the boss." James's eyes twinkled. "You hit the nail square on the head when you asked Hank which one of them rules the roost. She does. He's too busy tryin' to get rich. But I think you maybe made him see a blind spot. Sure as hell if he talks to her before that whiskey wears off there's goin' to be feathers flying. What'd you put the bottle away for?"

Pepperdine reluctantly brought it up again and watched the gunsmith take its contents dangerously near the bottom. As he was shoving the bottle away for the second time he cocked his head at Pepperdine. "You weaseled around an answer about the lad's paw as slippery as a greased pig."

Hugh frowned. "I had nothin' to tell him except what I said."

McGregor agreed with that. He was getting more mellow by the moment. He winked as he said, "A lie now'n then is good for the soul. In a good cause, Hugh. Only in a good cause. I'll bet you a new hat Hank's daughter don't ask the lad about his father, but if I'm wrong, what can he tell her?"

Hugh ignored the question to make a statement of his own. "That son of a bitch was in here yestiddy."

McGregor nodded. There was very little he missed. In fact, the roadway window in his shop had for years provided him with a view of the outside world. "He come into town with three mean-lookin' riders." McGregor paused, eyed the bottle thoughtfully, then made a statement that caused his friend's brows to shoot straight up. "An' his wife come along on the stage this morning. Did you know that? I can see you didn't. Well, I wish you'd empty that bottle."

Hugh emptied it and put it back beneath the counter. "How do you know it was his wife?"

"Because she come across from the corralyard to my shop an' asked me where she could find lodgings for a few days. She said her name was Harriet Barber. She also said she hadn't heard from her husband in a month and had to find him." James looked stonily at Pepperdine. "She said his name was Davy Barber an' when he left the ranch down in Arizona they wasn't speaking an' she wanted to see him real bad."

Hugh slowly carved a corner off his molasses-cured plug and fed it into his mouth on the cutting edge of the knife. "You sent her up to the roominghouse?"

"Yes."

"The story I heard was that she had a daughter when she married Davy."

McGregor shrugged. "She arrived alone. I don't know anythin' else about her. Except that she looked dog-tired."

"Did you tell her where Davy's cow camp is?"

"No. I don't volunteer information, specially if it's likely to cause trouble, an' that lady didn't impress me as someone's new wife who can't stand bein' separated from the love of her life. She looked as haggard as a person can be."

Hugh could believe that without ever having seen the woman. "Davy is trouble," he said, and related his exchange with Barber the day before over Hugh refunding some of the money Barber had given him last season to teach George a trade.

McGregor's comment about that was succinct and forthright. "I warned you. To my knowledge, up here in our country anyway, no one's ever come off very good that tangled with Davy Barber."

Their discussion was cut short when old Silas walked in with his face, neck, and half his shoulders protected from sunlight by that oversized hat he was rarely without. McGregor winked at Hugh, nodded curtly at the stage company's local boss, and walked diagonally across Main Street in the direction of his shop.

Silas was after his driving lines. Hugh had one set yet to mend but tossed the others atop the counter and watched Silas sort them until he could count each set. He then raised his little eyes with their muddy whites, and said, "One short."

"It's in the sewing horse right now. It'll be ready first thing in the morning."

Silas ran the repaired lines through his fingers, making an intent examination as he said, "You said they'd all be ready today."

Hugh let the irritation pass before replying. "I told you day after tomorrow, an' that'd be tomorrow."

Silas made his irritating sniffing sound as he finished examining the lines. "I'll pay when I get the other set," he told Pepperdine, flung the repaired lines over his shoulder, and got almost to the door before turning to

101

speak again. "One of the passengers who come in on my northbound this morning is Davy Barber's new wife."

Hugh nodded woodenly. "So I heard." He was turning toward the sewing horse when Silas spoke again. "When she opened her purse up in my office to pay the extra charge for an overload of baggage, she had a pearl-handled revolver in it."

Hugh shrugged, and after Silas had departed he went back to work for about fifteen minutes. Then he stopped and sat astraddle the sewing horse staring at the wall.

Lots of women traveling alone carried pistols. Probably most of them did, and more than likely Davy Barber's wife was like all those other ladies. But if McGregor was right in his judgment of the woman—and Hugh had yet to know James's judgment to be that wrong—she'd arrived in Sheridan distraught and seeking her husband, who, it seemed, had simply got his drive underway down at the ranch and had struck out without looking back.

Just how distraught was she? And what was the cause of her agitation? Anyone who was seriously upset and who was carrying a weapon was more likely to shoot someone than a person without those problems.

Hugh shed his apron, hiked down to the jailhouse, found the marshal gone, and went over to the cafe to see if anyone knew where he was.

One man knew because he boarded the lawman's animals. Reg Lee of the liverybarn told Hugh the marshal had gone out to investigate a horse theft southeast of town and most likely wouldn't return until evening or maybe not even until tomorrow morning.

Hugh went up to the gun shop, but the door was locked. McGregor was down at the cafe having supper. Hugh returned to his own shop, went out back, and, for lack of anything better to do, dumped the coffee grounds from his pot, scoured it inside and out with wet dirt, rinsed it thoroughly and returned to pour in the water. He dropped in a handful of beans and put it on the cold stove so it would be ready when he fired things up in the morning.

Then he went over to Rusty Morton's place for a nightcap. McGregor was over there. They took a bottle and two jolt glasses to a distant table, and Hugh explained his problem to the gunsmith. When he'd finished the story of his suspicion, he said, "If she's up there at the hotel waitin' for morning so's she can hire a buggy an' ride out there to shoot Barber, Fogarty's not goin' to know anything about it, specially if he don't get back until tomorrow."

James cogitated without lifting his jolt glass and fired up a powerful-smelling little nubbin of a pipe before delivering his judgment.

"It's not up to us, Hugh. An' privately I'd help harness the buggy horse and point out the way if I knew that's what she's up to."

Hugh rolled his eyes ceilingward. "What's in my craw has little to do with someone salivatin' Davy Barber. What's in my craw is whether he told her about havin' a catch colt up here, an' if he did . . ."

"Why would a man tell his wife somethin' like that?"

"Because it'd make him feel masculine. An' Davy's the kind that'd do it. Knowin' it would cause someone pain, he'd do it."

CHAPTER 13

The Spring Wind

WHEN THE TWO OLDER MEN FINALLY GOT TO BED without having settled anything, there was a bumbling, little wind blowing, a typical springtime series of chilly gusts that came from different directions with pauses between gusts. But by morning when they and the other inhabitants of Sheridan rolled out, it was a full-blown spring windstorm.

It did not let up all day. McGregor had to wad up some rags and force them beneath his roadway door to keep the grit out. Before the wind went on its way it would pile up some respectable drifts throughout town and knock about half the fruit blossoms off local trees.

Joe Fogarty, who had arrived in town late the previous night, had been bucking the wind through long hours of cold darkness when everyone else in Sheridan was asleep.

By the time he left his animal with Reg Lee's nightman and forced his way all the way up to the hotel—which was actually a roominghouse—to bed down, he was spitting grit and tired to the bone.

He did not appear down at the cafe until just about every bachelor or widower around town had already had breakfast and departed. Hugh saw him hiking down there, this time leaning slightly backward, because the wind was coming from the north.

Hugh watched George cutting new cheekpieces for a torn bridle as he removed his apron. "I'll be back directly," he told the youth, and got as far as the door before George spoke.

"I expect you know you caused a ruckus yesterday, Mr. Pepperdine."

Hugh was mildly perplexed. "I did?"

"Yep. Mr. Dennis an' his wife had a row in the office. His clerk went back there an' closed the door because they had customers."

"I caused it?"

"Yep. Seems he was over here talkin' to you, an' you got him a little smoked-up, so's when he got back to the store where she was waitin' to talk to him, he took her by the arm, marched her back there, and lit into her like the devil after a crippled saint." George eyed the older man. "I guess you told Mr. Dennis a lot of things because he quoted you as he liked to have blown her out of the store."

Hugh was relieved. "Oh, that. Well, we had a little talk is all. You'n his girl get things settled?"

"Pretty much. You better get along. We can talk later."

Hugh reached the cafe just as Joe Fogarty was attacking the first decent meal he'd had in a long while. As Hugh called for java and eased down beside him the lawman looked around with full cheeks, nodded, and went back to his meal. Pepperdine related what old Silas had said about his lady passenger with the gun in her purse.

Fogarty did not miss a single rhythmic chew until Hugh dropped his bombshell; then he stopped chewing, gazed at the older man, and said, "How do you know she's Davy's wife?"

"Because she told McGregor and Silas."

Fogarty went back to his meal, but with less enthusiasm now as he mulled over what he'd heard.

Finally, with the platter two-thirds empty, he shoved it away, pulled in the coffee cup, curled his hands around it, and said, "She'll have to hire a horse or a rig to reach Barber's camp."

Hugh wagged his head. "In this wind?"

"That'll depend on how bad she wants to see Davy, won't it? An' if she left McGregor feelin' that she was upset, why then, I got to expect the wind won't stop her."

Fogarty rose, spilled coins on the counter, and walked out of the cafe with Pepperdine on his heels.

Fogarty ignored the saddlemaker as he struck out southward in the direction of the liverybarn, leaning against the wind all the way.

Down there he ran into Reg Lee's scrawny dayman who was wearing a hat pulled half over his ears and a threadbare, old, buckskin coat that had enough grease stains down its front to feed a herd of mice for a week.

Reg was not around, and his dayman did not know where he'd gone, so Fogarty asked about a lady hiring either a rig or a saddle animal. The dayman shook his head. "Nope. In fact, since this damned wind started yestiddy we ain't hardly made bean money, an' I don't blame folks. Y'know, Marshal, when it's cold a man can figure a way to get warm, an' when it's real hot he can usually find a creek to get cool in, but nobody's ever given me one good remedy for what wind does to a man's nerves."

Fogarty started back northward, leaning this time all the way up to the roominghouse. There he ran head-on into something he was completely unprepared for. The roominghouse proprietor, a disillusioned individual who found refuge from an embittered disposition in a line of empty bottles that would have reached from Sheridan down to Bordenton, wagged his head. "She was moanin' an' groanin' somethin' fierce, so I took her down to Henry Pohl. If she's fixin' to take off, I'd sooner she done it down there than up here. Folks dyin' in hotels gives 'em a bad name."

Fogarty said, "Show me her room," which the proprietor did without a qualm. He stood in the doorway watching as Marshal Fogarty ransacked the woman's single leather valise, looked among the pockets of the clothing she'd hung from wall pegs, and finally shouldered past into the hallway on his way back out into the wind.

Down at Dr. Pohl's place Henry's very handsome, buxom wife showed him to the parlor and would have gone to fetch her husband, but Joe sank into a chair, shook his head at her as he dropped his hat on the floor, and said, "Just let me set here for a spell, Eleanor. Where is he, across the alley?"

She nodded without either of them having to specify what "across the alley" meant. She offered Fogarty coffee as he was removing some papers from a pocket. He declined, and she left him alone.

There were four unpaid bills, two from someone who had sold Davy Barber six purebred redback bulls seven months before the date on the last bill. There was also a letter from this individual saying that, if he had to come all the way from Texas to collect, he was going to take someone's scalp back to Texas with him along with the money.

The fourth piece of paper was from a doctor in a place called Buttonwillow. It was also a bill. Along with it was a terse note in fine, Spencerian script that Fogarty had no difficulty reading. In fact, he read it three times. It said that someone named Christine was finally

107

beginning to respond to treatment, but that she would have to stay with the doctor for about another six weeks while her physical injuries healed. The doctor could make no predictions about her mental condition.

Fogarty shoved his legs out, solemnly gazed at scuffed boot toes, and scarcely noticed wind scrabbling among the eaves outside. Finally he picked up his hat, shoved the papers into a pocket, and went through the house and across the alley, where the wind had dust hanging in the air ten feet aboveground.

Henry was finishing an embalming. Smell of the preservative was strong despite cracks in the old shed's walls where wind passed in and out.

They had to speak loudly enough to be heard over the noise outside. As Henry dried both hands, then removed a rubber apron while studying his handiwork, he said, "If it's about the lady in the back bedroom, she's got a ninety-year-old heart." In the same detached manner as he had spoken, Dr. Pohl pulled up the old piece of canvas to hide the body he'd been working on as he continued, "in a forty-five-year-old body."

"Do you know who she is?"

"The feller who runs the roominghouse brought her down here before breakfast this morning. He said she'd signed his book as Harriet Barber then scratched that out and wrote 'Harriet Blake.' "

"Did you talk to her?"

"Just barely. Eleanor put her to bed. Maybe they talked, I don't know." Henry waved a hand toward the embalmed corpse on his worktable. "The funeral's this afternoon. I haven't had time to do anything else."

Fogarty eyed the outline beneath the length of old, soiled canvas. "Who was he?"

"An old hanger-on who lived in one of the tarpaper

108

shacks at the lower end of town. No one knew him by any name but Old Frank. He drank, kept to himself, and just went to sleep and didn't wake up. At least not here in Sheridan."

Henry tossed the towel aside, leaned back, and eyed Marshal Fogarty. "Is she Davy Barber's wife?"

"That's what she told Silas and McGregor. Her purse wasn't in her room up yonder."

Dr. Pohl pushed off the wall as he spoke. "She was clutching it like a newborn baby. Come along, I think Eleanor hung it on the back of the sick-room door."

As Henry passed Marshal Fogarty reached to grab an arm. "How bad off is she?"

Henry Pohl looked the lawman squarely in the face when he replied. "It's up to her and Providence. There's no medicine I know of that'll do much for a diseased heart. And I think she's been pushing herself hard lately, because she's run down in other ways, too. How bad off? Joe, maybe a couple of days, maybe six months, or if there is a miracle, a year, but if I was a betting man I'd bet on two days, at the most a week. Come along."

Ordinarily Fogarty could not get out of that gruesome shed fast enough. Ordinarily, too, he'd have been conscious of the buffeting wind as they crossed to the rear of the house.

He was pulling off his hat for the second time in Henry Pohl's parlor as Eleanor agreed to get the woman's purse and departed. Dr. Pohl went into his operating room and returned with two glasses of amber whiskey. Both men emptied the glasses without a nod or a word. When the doctor's wife returned, Fogarty accepted the large, worn, old cowhide purse and moved toward better light as he opened it.

109

The gun was there. He lifted it out under the eyes of the Pohls, put it aside, and dug among the clutter of a handbag. He brought forth a small blue bottle that Henry Pohl took from him and a sealed letter with no address on the envelope.

Henry handed back the small blue vial with a wry look. "Standard stuff, Joe. It's supposed to ease their minds, which it may do, but it has absolutely no effect on a diseased heart."

Fogarty went closer to a window, opened the sealed envelope, read in absolute silence, reread the letter, folded it with a stone-set expression, and shoved the letter into a pocket. He raised his eyes to the doctor and his handsome wife. "Can I see her?"

Eleanor Pohl hesitated. "She's sleeping, Marshal. I suppose we can waken her."

Henry said nothing; he was wearing his detached look again. Joe Fogarty put on his hat. "Let her sleep. I'll be back later, when she's rested."

After he had departed, Dr. Pohl picked up the little gun Joe hadn't taken with him, examined it, and put it on a sideboard behind the massively framed daguerreotype of some people whose attire signified that they had belonged to an earlier era.

As he turned, his wife had a question. "I tried, Henry; maybe you could have made her talk. She seems very ill, doesn't she?"

"She is very ill, Ellie. Did she say anything to you?"

"Very little. She asked where she was and why I was putting her to bed. She said something about someone named Christine then went to sleep."

Henry nodded without meeting his wife's gaze and took the pair of sticky little glasses to the kitchen to be rinsed before they were returned to his operating room.

In his line of work it paid to keep a bottle handy; six out of every ten patients he patched together in his operating room required nothing stronger than whiskey. Also, because he knew the real effects of a genuine painkiller called laudanum, he did not use it if there was any way to avoid doing so.

The wind rattled windows and doors. Eleanor said it was fraying her nerves. Henry smiled at her. "You'll have plenty of company before it blows itself out. I've got to make some calls." He kissed her cheek and went to the hall stand for his hat, coat, and little black satchel.

James McGregor saw Joe Fogarty leave the Pohl's residence first, and about fifteen minutes later Henry Pohl went past, head bowed, clutching his satchel.

Hugh also saw them. At closer range, in fact, because they passed by on his side of the roadway, and there was less dust to interfere with his view.

He hadn't told George why he'd gone out earlier, and when the lad looked up from the worktable as Dr. Pohl passed, he said, "Hell of a day to have a baby, Mr. Pepperdine."

Hugh agreed that it was; that, in fact, it was a hell of a day for just about anything. Evidently George had missed seeing Marshal Fogarty go past.

His apprentice was in a mood of quiet amiability. He forgot about the doctor passing almost before he bent down over the harness bridle, as he said, "I guess folks can change a lot without even realizin' they're doin' it, can't they?"

Hugh eyed the muscular back of the tall youth before replying. "Seems to me that's goin' on all a man's life. Sometimes he can feel it, and sometimes he can't. You got somethin' on your mind?"

George did not look up when he answered. "I felt real

bad about Mr. Barber refusin' to take me down to Arizona with the drive."

"What did he say about it?"

"That he didn't need me down there, that I wouldn't like the country, an' for a fact I was beginnin' to feel at home up here."

Hugh was frowning at the youth's back. "My impression was that you hadn't wanted to go down there."

George looked around. "Is that what he told you?"

"Yes."

George bent over his work again. "That's what he kept tellin' me, too. He talked himself blue in the face about me stayin' up here an' learnin' a trade. I wanted to go with him, but after he told what rough country that was down yonder, I said I wanted to stay up here. So maybe what he said was the truth—as far as he knew."

Hugh scratched his thatch, raised and dropped his shoulders and let the subject die. For a damned fact there were times when trying to figure people out was impossible.

CHAPTER 14

A Man Can't Be Two Places At Once

ABOUT THE TIME EVERYONE WAS READY TO CHEW nails and spit rust, the wind died. Not overnight, which was customary, but in broad daylight. One minute it was howling, the next moment it was down to a whimper, and half an hour later the only reminder that it had been blowing was the dust. It was in the air, in the stores, piled on the lee sides of structures, and in the food folks ate.

But with its passing the inconveniences were forgotten. Even old Silas Browning let his face crack a little.

Joe Fogarty was down at the smithy, arranging for one of his horses to have new shoes and for the other one to have a trim and a reset, when the northbound coach up from Bordenton rattled through silence, dust, and sunshine on its way to the corralyard.

There were no passengers, just some light freight, which suited Silas down to the ground. Light freight paid as well, and he didn't have to listen to complaints.

Marshal Fogarty had been avoiding the harness shop for what he considered an excellent reason. He knew something that would make old Pepperdine explode in all directions.

He should have avoided the gun shop, too, but in the course of a stroll up through town past Morton's saloon on the east side of Main Street, he encountered James McGregor diligently adding to the dust by vigorously sweeping out his place of business. The moment Marshal Fogarty appeared James stopped sweeping to say, "You know about Davy Barber's wife bein' up at the roominghouse?"

Instead of explaining that she was no longer up there, Fogarty nodded his head and would have continued on his way, but McGregor had one more thing to say. "Buster Henning come by early this morning on his way down to get the mail an' left an old gun to have it fixed. He said he's been havin' trouble with Davy's drift lately, an' when he rode over to see if Davy wouldn't do somethin' about it, Davy told him if Buster didn't like Davy's cattle on his grass it was up to him to turn them back, it wasn't up to Davy to hunt for them."

Fogarty nodded woodenly.

McGregor moved slightly to expectorate before finishing. "Buster's mad as a hornet. Did he find you?"

"No. Was he lookin' for me?"

"Said he was goin' to see about gettin' you to ride out there and yank some slack out of Davy, because if you don't there's goin' to be trouble."

Joe Fogarty sighed audibly. "I didn't see him. But then I didn't roll out until past sunup and then some. Is he still in town?"

McGregor didn't know so he jutted his jaw. "You might ask Hugh. Him an' Buster are pretty close, have been for years. Buster don't come to town but that he swaps lies in the harness shop."

Joe looked across the road. He had what he felt was the best of all reasons for not going over there, but he went anyway, convinced that Davy Barber was becoming more difficult each year until this season he was making a dangerous mistake. Buster Henning was a big, fat man who liked to laugh, easygoing, fair as the day was long. But he'd had deeded land out there before Davy'd commenced to drive north for the early grass every year, and Joe Fogarty had heard some grisly stories about Henning's violent reactions to other people who had goaded him.

George was at the worktable when Fogarty walked in. He glanced up, nodded, and jerked his head to indicate that Hugh was on through the shop in his room. Joe's brows lightly knit. "Not sick is he?"

George's reply was dry. "Not so's you'd notice. He had a bottle under the counter, and it was empty, so he went back there to dig out another one."

Fogarty went back to the closed door and knocked. Hugh, supposing it was his apprentice, said, "You better stay up front in case someone comes in."

Fogarty opened the door. Hugh twisted to look around, showing an annoyed expression. Fogarty ignored the look. "James told me Buster Henning was around this morning."

Hugh had found the bottle and put it atop the upended wooden horseshoe keg beside his cot as he replied. "Yeah, but he didn't stop in. He waved as he rode out of town is all. You want to see him?"

Fogarty looked around for a safe chair, found one that was less rickety than the others, and sat down. He shoved back his hat and eyed Hugh Pepperdine. "Yeah. Davy's free-grazing, and Buster don't like it."

"He could run Davy off."

Fogarty had to swivel one hip to prevent a long, wooden splinter from gouging his underside. "The way I heard it, Buster complained an' Davy told him if he don't want Davy's cattle on his grazin' grounds it's up to Buster to get them off."

Hugh sat down. "I thought they got along."

Fogarty shrugged about that. "I did too, until this season anyway. . . . That lady you told me about with the gun in her purse?"

"Yeah. Davy's wife."

"She's at Henry's place pretty damned ill. Bad heart."

Hugh wagged his head. "That's too bad." His compassion, while genuine, did not last long. He grimaced at the lawman. "I don't have to live around the son of a bitch, an' sometimes when he's in here I get heartburn."

Fogarty did not return the smile. "Henry gives her maybe a week."

"Well, hell, she really is bad off then. You reckon someone ought to go out an' tell Davy? Whatever's

115

between them, him being her husband he'd ought to be told, hadn't he?"

Marshal Fogarty eyed his boot toes. "I'm goin' out there first thing in the morning. Davy's gettin' crankier as the years pass. That's not open range. Buster's got deeds to every bit of his grazing land. So has Davy." His steady eyes came up slowly. "She's not his wife. Where'd you hear that she was?"

Hugh was startled. By now he'd been thinking of Davy as being married for so long he could not discard the idea of the spur of the moment. "As I recollect, Rusty said he saw somethin' about it in a newspaper." Hugh paused, looked steadily at the larger, younger man, and asked a question. "Are you plumb certain? Don't seem likely they'd put somethin' like that in a newspaper, even in Arizona, if it wasn't true."

Joe Fogarty sat gazing across the dingy little room without speaking for a while. He relented about his reason for avoiding Pepperdine, fished out a crumpled envelope, and tossed it on the cot.

Hugh retrieved it, spread it flat, puckered his brow, and formed words with his lips as he read. When he was two-thirds of the way through he looked across at the lawman. Neither of them said a word, not even for a few moments after Hugh had passed the paper back to Fogarty.

Then he didn't explode, as Fogarty had expected. He didn't even look angry. He leaned down, clasped both hands, and studied the floor for a long time. Might have gone on studying it but Marshal Fogarty leaned to arise. Then Hugh said, "Somebody's goin' to shoot that son of a bitch, Joe."

Fogarty was standing up when he replied. "Not you, partner. The reason I showed you the letter is because I

116

can't be two places at once. I got to go out there tomorrow and try'n head off someone gettin' shot, and I need someone to go down to Bordenton where they got a telegraph office and send off a request to the doctor down in Buttonwillow for verification from him of what's in this letter and a letter I found in the woman's purse about the girl's health and injuries. . . . Hugh?"

Pepperdine continued to perch on the edge of his cot, gazing up at the lawman. "Someone should have shot that—"

"Never mind! I want to know if what's in this letter is the truth."

"Can't you ask the woman?"

"I doubt that she'd tell me straight out. Not if she's got it in mind to settle with Davy herself. An' she just might not tell me anyway, if she's as sick as Henry says. She might not even be alive when I get back tomorrow evening. An then there's something else. What's in this letter is somethin' I just don't see a woman tellin' to a total stranger, badge or no badge. . . Hugh? First southbound in the morning so's we can meet tomorrow night with whatever answer you get back?"

Pepperdine nodded and shoved up off the cot to lead the way back through the shop to the sunbright roadway where he lowered his voice so George could not hear from back at the worktable. "Supposin' it's all true?"

Fogarty glanced up the roadway where a grizzled old cowman and his nearly as-weathered old wife were driving into town as proud as peacocks of a top buggy so new that dust hadn't hardly settled on it yet. It had a hinge around the top and bright yellow running gear. It also had something else that was as yet fairly uncommon; not steel tires: hard rubber ones.

Without lowering his eyes Fogarty answered quietly.

117

"I'm not sure."

Hugh's eyes sparked. "Well, I sure am." He turned. "See you tomorrow night at the jailhouse."

Hugh went all the way back to his lean-to and would have returned to the shop clutching the bottle if it hadn't occurred to him that he needed a jolt or two after what he'd just read and what he'd been listening to. He fought the cap off, tipped his head, lowered the bottle, recapped it, and went out into the shop with a decided warmth moving all the way down his slightly saddle-warped legs to his feet.

George watched him shove the bottle under the counter and held up the finished headstall as he said, "You expect this'll please 'em, Mr. Pepperdine?"

Hugh had to avert his face and belch soundlessly before replying. "It's as good a job as I ever saw, son. To my way of thinkin' it'd please anyone on earth except Silas Browning, and that old screwt won't even be pleased at the Resurrection unless he can find tarnish on someone's halo."

George draped the completed article from a wooden peg in the wall and moved to wipe his hands with considerable care, an exercise Hugh had of late come to understand meant that George was going to ask if it'd be all right if he quit work for the day.

Before that happened he told his apprentice he'd be gone all day tomorrow and would take it kindly if George would mind the shop and not close up before sundown.

George agreed, and eyed the older man with interest but did not ask the obvious question because the one on the tip of his tongue was of vastly more personal concern to him.

"Mind if I leave for the day now?"

118

Hugh dropped a roguish wink as he answered. "Don't mind at all. There's nothin' here that can't wait another day or two. George? You don't have to answer if you don't want to but—by any chance have you two got around to makin' serious plans yet?"

The tall, powerfully built youth did not turn a hair. Last year he would have burned fiery red and stared at his feet. "Sort of. Charlotte's folks want the weddin' to be at the church an' the reception to be at their house."

Hugh nodded about that. The Dennis residence was one of the finest around, and perhaps because Hank was able to get a lot of fine furnishings at wholesale, him being a merchant and all, it was definitely the best furnished. "That'll give you'n the girl somethin' to recollect as long as you live."

". . . An' I want you to stand up with me, Mr. Pepperdine."

Hugh felt the lump growing in his throat until he thought it'd suffocate him. "Son. That's a real honor. Maybe if you asked Charlotte's father . . . ?"

"No. I told them I wanted you. Mr. Dennis thought it was a fine idea. So did Charlotte."

Hugh waited, but the lad stopped right there. Hugh looked gravely across the counter at George with an expression so bland it couldn't have been genuine, and it wasn't. Inside he was gloating over Charlotte's mother not being able to move the lad off center about this, that damned old blacksmith's daughter who'd married Hank and his store and hadn't been able to touch solid earth with her big feet ever since.

"Mr. Pepperdine?"

"I don't know what to say, son. Of course I'll do it." He'd have to buy a new suit; his regular go-to-meeting suit was turning slightly green in places. "You know,

George, I never been a best man before."

The youth's steady, dead-level gaze did not waver, but his color heightened slightly. "Me'n Charlotte came up with somethin', if you don't mind, and providin' we have kids. First boy'll be Hugh Pepperdine Jefferson."

That, by gawd, would give Charlotte's mother fits, but at this particular moment in Hugh's life he didn't think of that. He would later, though, as he and McGregor were nursing two ten-cent glasses of popskull over at the saloon. Right now Hugh had to turn away and gaze out the front window as he replied. "I got to think back, boy, but right offhand I think that's the nicest thing anyone ever said to me." He did not dare turn. "You better go. It don't pay to keep folks waiting."

He watched the youth head through bright sunshine as he eased down a little unsteadily on the old worktable. Damned dust was still in the air. He had to swab at his eyes. Or maybe it was that drink he'd had before fetching the bottle into the shop. Well, whatever in hell it was, it not only made his eyes water, it also made them burn. And that damned lump in his throat didn't dissolve right away either.

He pushed the bandanna back into a pocket, arose with a growl, and went to the counter to take a deep swallow from the bottle under there. At that exact moment Silas Browning under his parasol of a hat came stamping in for that set of driving lines that hadn't been finished the day before.

Silas stopped stone-still in his tracks, his eyes came up to a glowing simmer, and without a word or a nod he about-faced and went stamping back the way he had come.

Hugh shoved the bottle back out of sight, leaned on his counter, and laughed until more tears came.

CHAPTER 15

Some Surprises

MCGREGOR WAS FINISHING BREAKFAST AT THE CAFE when a pair of dusty, faded rangemen came in slapping at their britches with shapeless old hats. They were both young men, cleanshaven, pleasant and hungry. As they dropped down on the bench beside McGregor the nearest man turned with a smile and said, "You ever wonder if there wasn't an easier way to serve the Lord than starin' at the rear end of cattle from the back of a horse?"

James replied that he hadn't given it much thought and besides he was a gunsmith not a stockman.

The cowboys gave their order to the slipper-shod cafeman and leaned, hands clasped, looking around. "Folks eat late around here, don't they?" one of them said to McGregor, and as before, he was noncommital.

"Most likely about the same as they do anywhere." He eyed the younger men. Both were stalwart, worn and weathered, and both wore sidearms as though part of their morning ritual was to pull on their britches and shellbelts simultaneously. "You boys new to the country?" McGregor asked.

The one farthest down the counter replied. "We won't be as soon as we finish deliverin' some Durham bulls to a feller named Davy Barber. We come with the animals." At McGregor's look of wary interest the rider explained further. "Mr. Barber contracted for these bulls, fifteen of 'em, before he headed north some time back, an' we agreed to deliver 'em up here for regular wages if he'd keep us on through the season. You know

121

where Mr. Barber's camp is?"

McGregor knew, had known for years, but true to his principle about giving out information, his reply was different than it could have been. "The best feller to give you directions would be Joe Fogarty over at the jailhouse, or maybe the folks at the general store. Where you got the bulls?"

The cowboy jerked his head. "Down at the public corrals." The cowboy grinned. "A fat man down there didn't like the idea. He said them corrals was for horses not cattle."

"But you left 'em there anyway?"

"Cost us two silver dollars."

The cafeman appeared with breakfast platters, the cowboys went to work on them, and McGregor paid up and left the cafe.

The jailhouse had not been unlocked yet this morning. McGregor consulted his pocket watch about that, made a disapproving grunt, and went up the same side of Main Street as far as the harness works, where George Jefferson was pressing a template against moist leather with one hand and outlining it with a pencil using the other hand.

At the gunsmith's inquiring gaze Hugh's apprentice said, "He isn't here, didn't say where he was goin', but he might not be back until late."

James leaned on the counter, waiting until the pattern had been traced, then said, "When he gets back tell him I was lookin' for him."

George nodded while replacing the pattern on its wall peg. "Anythin' I can do, Mr. McGregor?"

James thought about that for a moment before speaking. "Some cowboys arrived in town with Durham bulls for Davy Barber. Got 'em down at the public corrals until they can rest up and head for his camp."

George turned. "How many?"

"Fifteen."

George nodded about that. "Last season when I was ridin' with him he said he was goin' to have to replace some old bulls; they didn't go lookin' for bulling cows, they hunted up shady places and stayed there."

McGregor accepted this trivia and asked if George had seen Marshal Fogarty this morning. When George said he hadn't, James went over across the road to his own shop, strapped a greasy apron into place, stirred some life into the coals beneath the coffeepot, and went looking for his glasses before examining the gun Buster Henning had left. And swore. Damned stockmen anyway. When they needed a tool to pry up a rock or to twist wire tight or to drive a loose horseshoe nail, they used their guns.

McGregor clamped the weapon into his vise, lighted a lamp to enhance visibility, and got down to sight between the rear and front sights. He swore again with the same degree of feeling as he straightened up. Rebarreling a Colt wasn't particularly difficult if a man had the implements but it was unnecessary in nine cases out of ten, unless the gun barrel had been used as this one had—as a lever.

A tall, sloped-shouldered, older rangeman, weathered, with a perpetual squint and a dusting of gray around the temples appeared in the doorway. James thought he'd seen him before but couldn't place the man until he walked over to the counter, smiled, and said, "Jess Bell, rangeboss for Davy Barber." Then McGregor remembered. He'd never done any business with the hard-eyed, brown, leathery-hided individual, but he'd seen him around town over the years.

123

"How are you? It's been a while."

The rangeboss nodded while eyeing the gun with the bent barrel. "Harnessmaker ain't around, I guess."

"His apprentice is over there."

Bell continued to eye the old six-gun. "Yeah. I seen him through the winder, but I was lookin' for Pepperdine." The hard, light-brown eyes came back to McGregor's face. "You'n him peerin' through the same knothole an' all, I figured you'd be able to tell me where I could find him."

James gave a candid reply. "I was lookin' for him, too, a while back. The lad said he'd be back tonight. That's all I know."

The rangeman nodded slowly, turned, and walked out of the shop, leaving James with an uncomfortable feeling, but it didn't last. He went over to start on the Henning gun.

Later, with some dogs on the west side of town raising hell and propping it up, McGregor went as far as the doorway to look around.

There was a trail of dust about a half mile west of town where two riders were having difficulty chasing town dogs back where they belonged and lining out about fifteen fighting Durham bulls that the dogs had worked up into a battling mood.

Evidently someone had told those men where Barber's cow camp was. McGregor went back to work and was not interrupted again until late in the evening. He was lighting a lamp in the center of the shop, heard a northbound coach coming, and turned to watch it pass.

Hugh Pepperdine was on it!

James finished with the lamp, shed his apron, and considered the repaired six-gun. It'd take that darned fool who owned it only until the next time he was riding out without any tools and needed a pry bar or a hammer to bend it, enough so's the bullets would go around corners when he fired it.

A horseman trooped past on a tired horse. McGregor, ready to cross the road to the harness works, stopped in his tracks. The rider was Marshal Fogarty, and from the looks of that horse he hadn't gone out to admire the wildflowers.

He stood briefly, watching Joe Fogarty ride all way down to Lee's barn and turn in, then crossed over to the harness shop where George was rolling a pair of pigeon-wing skirts into a moist croaker sack to soften until tomorrow morning when he would work them up.

George shook his head when James was in the doorway. "He hasn't returned yet."

James teetered a moment then headed for the cafe, but when he got down there Hugh was not among the local feeders. Since it was time for his own supper, James went to the counter, nodded unsmilingly at the cafeman who nodded back the same way, and ordered his dinner. When the coffee arrived, he ignored it, because he'd been drinking coffee all day.

Daylight was fading. Here and there merchants were either lighting lamps or locking up for the day. McGregor did not see the light in the jailhouse until he'd finished eating and was counting out small coins for the cafeman.

He already knew Joe Fogarty had returned, but he strolled over there anyway with nothing to say except that he was interested in the whereabouts of his old friend.

They were both in there, looking tired and tucked up. Each of them was nursing a cup of black coffee, and when James walked in they eyed him with no noticeable enthusiasm. James nodded to Marshal Fogarty and addressed Pepperdine. "Davy Barber's rangeboss was lookin' for you this afternoon."

"What did you tell him?"

"Nothing. I went by the shop this morning, an' George said you was gone. That's about all I knew."

Hugh shoved his long legs out as he asked another question. "Did he say what he wanted?"

"No. Is there any coffee left, Joe?"

Fogarty jutted his jaw toward the pot atop the little stove. "Help yourself."

McGregor didn't want the coffee; he'd been pretty well coffeed out even before supper, but he filled a cup anyway.

When he faced around neither of the other men were looking at him, or, for that matter, at each other. McGregor tested the brew, found it not too hot, and took a couple of swallows. He studied the harnessmaker and the town marshal and asked when the funeral was going to be.

Hugh's eyes came up and lingered impassively on the gunsmith until Marshal Fogarty leaned to push a piece of paper to the edge of his desk.

McGregor crossed over, picked it up in one hand—still holding his cup in the other hand—glanced up just once, then reread the letter. He tossed it back atop the desk, crossed to a wall bench, and sat down over there, looking from one of them to the other.

Fogarty wasn't finished. He shoved a yellowish paper to the edge of the desk, and said, "Read that one, too. Hugh brought that one back from Bordenton."

McGregor crossed to the desk, read the telegram, began to get a deep vertical line between his tufted brows even before placing the second piece of paper

126

beside the other one atop the desk, and finally spoke. "That's a hangin' matter." He returned to the bench still holding the cup but no longer aware of its existence. "That's where you been all day, Hugh, down yonder sending a telegram to that feller in Buttonwillow?" He did not allow Pepperdine time to reply, and now, finally, he put the cup on the bench. "Joe, you'll need more than just your badge if you go out there to bring Davy in. There was a couple of young fellers passin' through with some Durham bulls for Barber, and I don't expect they'll get involved, but I can tell you straight out that Davy's rangeboss, the feller I told you was lookin' for Hugh, is trouble four ways from the middle. From what I've heard over the years, Davy don't hire 'em unless they're mean an' willing."

Joe Fogarty drained his cup and shoved it into a pile of untidy papers on his desk. But it was Hugh who spoke next. "What kind of a man does somethin' like that? All the way back here this afternoon I was tryin' to find an answer to that. Bad enough he beat the woman; that's enough to get a man shot in most places I been, but what he did to a sixteen-year-old girl . . ."

McGregor slapped his legs and shot up to his feet. "Let it be known around town, and Joe'll have a posse ridin' with him loaded for bear—or lynching."

Fogarty asked if James had seen Henry Pohl today. When McGregor shook his head, Fogarty struggled up to his feet, reaching for his hat. "I'm goin' up there. If that woman will tell me in her words that these things happened, I'll round up that posse, James."

The harnessmaker and gunsmith were left alone in the marshal's office. Hugh shoved up straighter in the chair, shook his head at McGregor, and said, "Beat the woman. That's likely got somethin' to do with her being

127

sick and all right now. But draggin' that screamin' girl into the root cellar an' doin' what he did, then beatin' her afterwards . . . She told 'em down in Buttonwillow Davy'd been drinking. But that don't cut any ice."

McGregor recalled the list of injuries mentioned in the telegram and settled back against the wall before speaking. "A little more an' he'd have beat her to death. When her mother came down there with a stove poker and hit Davy with it so's the girl could escape, it's a damned wonder he didn't take the poker an' kill 'em both with it. . . . Hugh, you had supper?"

"James, I haven't been hungry all day, but I sure could do with some whiskey."

McGregor arose, but Hugh, who came up more slowly, said, "My shop, not the saloon. I don't feel much like listenin' to a bunch of whinnying idiots tonight."

When they got up there, George was waiting. He barely more than grinned at Hugh before departing with long strides for the opposite side of Main Street.

As Hugh was unscrewing the cap behind the counter he said, "Joe went out there today to tell Davy to stop lettin' his cattle drift over onto Buster." Hugh paused to hoist the bottle, swallow, and shove it toward McGregor. "Davy told him it's always been open-range law that if someone don't want someone else's cattle grazin' over them, they got to keep them out, the owner don't have to."

McGregor held the bottle without lifting it as he regarded his friend. "He's right, Hugh. That's the law in any open-range country."

Pepperdine watched James raise and lower the bottle. "Davy told him somethin' else. He said I owed him money because George learnt the trade within a couple

128

of months, an' he paid me to keep him on for eight months."

James snorted. No one learned any trade in a couple of months, not even someone as talented as George was. But there was something that had been bothering McGregor ever since George had gone to work with Hugh. His brow furrowed as he looked at Pepperdine while speaking. "There's somethin' I never been able to square with what I know about Davy Barber. Up until now I sort of figured he helped the lad because, like I read once, nobody's all bad. Later on when I knew what their relationship was, I figured Davy had a soft spot for his son even if he wouldn't admit they was related."

Hugh was going through pockets for his chewing tobacco when he said, "Soft part your butt, James. Joe listened to the talk up there today, rode out with a couple of the riders, and come back with what he figures was behind Davy's generosity last summer. First off, that lady up at Henry's place isn't married to Davy, but her daughter, the one Davy dang near killed in the root cellar, was Davy's daughter." At McGregor's surprised look, Hugh said, "Another catch colt. Fogarty figured Davy couldn't risk havin' George trail down to the home ranch and meet that woman an' her daughter, because if George found out the girl was a catch colt, he was likely to start thinking about his own paw. He's a smart lad; how long you expect it would have been before he figured out the answer to that secret his mother wouldn't tell him—especially after she knew he was workin' for Davy? She didn't want her child hanged for murderin' his father. She knew sure as I'm standin' here that George would figure out who his father was."

CHAPTER 16

On Into the Night

MARSHAL FOGARTY SAW THEM IN THE HARNESS SHOP as he was returning from Henry Pohl's place and walked in to make a tight little head-nod as he raised a hand to decline Hugh's offer of the bottle.

James said, "Well?"

"She wasn't married to him, but she told me she told a newspaper down there that she was, because she didn't want her daughter to know the truth, which was simply that after Davy got her pregnant he rode off and never came back."

Hugh frowned. "He must have come back, Joe, otherwise how'd she come to be at his ranch?"

"It wasn't her, it was her daughter. She met Davy in some town down there, he commenced courtin' her—"

"His own daughter, for crissake?"

"He didn't know she was his daughter. That's when the trouble started. When she brought her maw along the time she went out to his ranch, Davy went wild; locked 'em in the house, got to drinkin', sent his riders into town, and went back to the house. He screamed at them they'd deliberately trapped him, an' he'd teach 'em a lesson. It was bad, real bad. When the woman was tellin' me all this she was cryin' like a little kid, an' Eleanor Pohl ran me off."

Hugh extended the bottle with a stiff arm, and this time they all had a drink. Fogarty studied the older men and warned them. "I know what you're thinkin', but don't you even make out like you're goin' to try it."

James swung blue eyes the color of ice to the

lawman's face. "Why not?"

"Because . . . You damned well know why not. Because the law'll take care of it."

McGregor's craggy face settled into lines of dogged opposition. "The law! Joe, I've seen the law work for more years than you are old, and it's a plumb failure eight out of ten times."

Fogarty's eyes glowed smokily. "James, right or wrong the law's what we got to live by."

McGregor snorted derisively. "You're old enough to know better, Joe. The law's for fee lawyers, politicians, an' other manipulators. I just told you it's wrong more'n it's right. An' I'll tell you somethin' else. I learned this over more'n fifty years: There's almost no comparison between your book-law and justice."

Hugh and the marshal gazed at McGregor over an interval of silence. Fogarty was obdurate, but Hugh Pepperdine slowly fished around for his plug, silent and pensive. After he got his cud settled and the lawman was preparing to speak, Hugh beat him to it.

"That's enough. There's plenty of trouble to go around without us makin' more. Joe, are you goin' after Davy?"

Fogarty's smouldering gaze left McGregor's face with an effort. "Yes."

"You got a charge against him?"

"Assault. Criminal assault."

McGregor snorted again, and this time Hugh fixed him with a stare for a long moment, then spoke to the town marshal again. "How many men's he got out there?"

"Six or eight. Don't worry, I'll get up a posse."

Hugh shifted his cud before replying to that. "An' ride out there loaded for bear so's they'll see you

131

comin' for a mile?"

Fogarty reddened. "You don't have to go."

"Neither do you, if you use your head." Both men looked at Hugh. "Get him to come here, Joe. Right here in town."

"How?"

"Well . . . I don't know, but—"

McGregor swore as he interrupted the harnessmaker. "If those riders deliverin' Davy's bulls was still in town we could use them to get him down here."

Fogarty's comment about that was tart. "But they aren't still here."

Hugh was beginning to form a rough idea. "Well, last summer he left a pile of old harness with me to be patched up. He said he'd come around for it this summer. Suppose I send word to him that it's ready, an' he can pick it up any time he's in town."

James was stuffing a foul little pipe as he was nodding his head. Marshal Fogarty went over to shake the coffeepot then put it down without filling a cup. "You got in mind sendin' your apprentice out there?"

That idea hadn't occurred to Pepperdine, and he did not like it. "Not on your tintype. Someone else. Maybe that rangeboss of his that was around town today lookin' for me. Maybe that's it, maybe he wanted to know about the harness."

"Sure as hell he's not still in town," McGregor stated, firing up his little pipe.

Hugh shrugged. "If that's what he wanted, he'll be back. I'll tell him his boss ought to look at the work before he takes it. Somethin' anyway that'll lure Davy down here."

George Jefferson walked in out of the darkness, paused in surprise at what obviously was some kind of serious palaver, then smiled self-consciously as he said, "Good evening." He would have walked right on through to his room off the back of the building if Hugh hadn't spoken to him.

"Have a nice evenin' did you?"

George turned. The older men were gazing at him without smiling. "Real nice. I'd better turn in. Good night."

They watched him walk toward the back of the shop. Fogarty was faintly frowning and looked at Hugh for an explanation. Pepperdine lowered his voice. "He's been sparkin' Hank Dennis's girl."

Joe's eyes widened. "I didn't know that."

"They're goin' to get married."

"The hell! I sure didn't know anything about that."

McGregor was tamping his pipe bowl with a callused thumbpad so he had to speak around a pipe stem. "You been busy with other things."

Fogarty straightened up. "I'm wore out. See you gents tomorrow," he said and left the harness shop hiking in the direction of the roominghouse.

McGregor went as far as the roadway door to expectorate and peer northward at the diminishing figure of the lawman. As he was turning back he said, "He must be tired. He forgot about makin' his last round of town before turnin' in."

Pepperdine did not want any further discussion about Joe Fogarty. "You care for another drink?"

"No thanks."

Hugh put the bottle on the undercounter shelf and leaned there, gazing at his old friend. "I got a hunch that even if we can chum Davy down here, arrestin' him isn't goin' to be all that easy. Knowin' his disposition like I do, I can tell you he don't have enough sense not to fight a buzz saw."

That reasoning left the gunsmith unaffected. "If folks knew what he did to that young girl an' her mother, he wouldn't have to worry about just a buzz saw. . . . I'm goin' home, too. See you in the morning."

Hugh lingered in the shop for a while, leaning there and going back over everything he'd learned today and everything that had been discussed. Around him, Sheridan was quiet. Even the town dogs weren't raising a ruckus for a change.

He jettisoned his chew and was straightening up off the counter, when a whispery little sound of leather over wood made him look toward the doorway.

The man leaning there smiling was as tall as Hugh but quite a bit younger. Hugh was seventy; the man grinning out of the dark at him was probably about forty-five. His skin was weathered dark; there was a sprinkling of gray at his temples. His pants and shirt were faded, his boots were scuffed, the work-roughened hands hooked in the shellbelt were strong and supple.

Hugh recognized him on sight. He was Barber's rangeboss, the man who had been looking for Hugh earlier in the day. That barely registered with the harnessmaker as they gazed at one another, because it was late and dark; no one waited this long to find someone unless their reason for doing so was deadly serious. Or maybe just deadly.

He'd heard rumors about Jess Bell. He'd heard similar whispers about other men who rode for Davy Barber. The hair was beginning to rise on the back of Hugh's neck as the leaning man made a quiet statement.

"Davy didn't send me. I come on my own, Pepperdine."

"About the mended harness?" Hugh asked.

"No. About the money you owe Davy. All he said was that if I collect it, I can keep it. Davy don't like folks takin' advantage of him. You can understand that. Nobody likes bein' takin' advantage of, now, do they?"

Except for their voices the night was as quiet as the inside of a tomb, and since neither man was speaking loudly even those sounds did not carry far.

Hugh considered the lanky, sun-bronzed, leaning man, who was still faintly smiling. Hugh could almost smell the trouble that was coming. What he'd heard about Davy's rangeboss was that he could kill a fleeing antelope from the back of a running horse at two hundred yards. True or not, that kind of shooting was very impressive.

Hugh's nearest weapon was in his back room. He eyed Bell's holstered weapon. Even if he'd had his old six-gun right in front of him on the counter he probably wouldn't stand the chance of a snowball in hell against the lethally smiling lanky man leaning half in darkness, half in lamplight.

The rangeboss pulled up off the door frame. "Davy figures you owe him three hunnert dollars, Mr. Pepperdine."

Hugh's eyes sprang wide open. "Three hunnert . . . ? Hell, he only gave me one hunnert an' fifty to begin with."

"Well, he told me it was three hunnert, an' I don't expect to stand here until sunup arguin' about it with you. But just to keep thinks friendly an' all, you put a hunnert an' fifty on that counter, and we won't have no trouble." The smile widened slightly. "I'm a reasonable man, Mr. Pepperdine."

Hugh's tiredness had dropped away somewhere between the time he'd first seen the rangeboss leaning

135

in his doorway and the moment, which was now, when he had to decide on a course of action.

No one in their right mind who was unarmed—and many times even if they were armed—argued with an armed man like Barber's rangeboss who wore that kind of a little, humorless, lethal smile.

"I don't have a hunnert an' fifty dollars on me," Hugh stated, saw the deadly smile begin to fade, saw Jess Bell's muscular right hand begin to close into a gun-drawing claw, and uttered the only words he thought might save his life. "I got forty-five dollars in my purse. I got another hunnert in a coffee can in my back room."

For a space of about five seconds after Hugh had spoken and before the rangeboss replied, the silence lingered; then a sound that was foreign to the men staring at one another interrupted everything. It was made by oily steel moving over oily steel from somewhere behind the man in the doorway.

Hugh wasn't breathing as the rangeboss perceptibly stiffened but otherwise did not move. His eyes were big and fixed on Pepperdine.

The moment the man back there in roadway darkness spoke, Hugh sucked in a big breath and slowly exhaled it. Joe Fogarty!

"Cowboy, you put both hands atop your head and don't move. Don't even turn your head."

The rangeboss obeyed very slowly and did not turn, although Hugh would have bet new money he'd try to see who was behind him with a cocked six-gun.

Fogarty's big frame moved into the lamplight as he disarmed Jess Bell, stepped back, and holstered his own weapon. He was shoving the appropriated weapon into his waistband as he said, "I was makin' my last round of locked doors for the night and heard you talking,

136

cowboy. Now, we're goin' down to the jailhouse, where I'm goin' to lock you up an' feed the key to a turkey. You understand me? Turn around."

Hugh had gone from a prime participant to an onlooker without feeling the slightest sense of unhappiness about it. He watched the rangeboss turn slowly. He was no more astonished than Marshal Fogarty was when the rangeboss fired two lighting-fast fists. Both connected, both stung the lawman, but like a lot of thrown blows that were that fast, they lacked hurting power.

Fogarty was nevertheless forced to step off the plankwalk into the roadway, not by the force of the strikes but to get clear of more of those blurred-fast stinging fists and to overcome his astonishment at the suddenness, the almost desperate fury of the attack.

Hugh leaned so far over the counter to watch that there was some danger of him falling over it. He wasted half a minute getting around the counter heading for the doorway. He did not get there in time.

Joe Fogarty was a bear of a man. He could be hurt by brawling and he had been over the years but not by anyone whose sole fighting attribute was speed. And Joe was like a man with bricks in his fisted hands when he pawed to keep the rangeboss away until he was ready to seize the initiative. Hugh Pepperdine was halfway to the doorway when Fogarty appeared to stumble. When the rangeboss launched himself for the kill, he ran head-on into a fist moving like a battering ram.

Hugh heard the sound of knuckles grating past flesh and over bone, vaguely saw something out in the dark roadway flinging and jerking like something hanging from a clothesline in a high wind, but by the time he got out there the writhing wraith was lying on its face, half

137

on the duckboards, half in the manured roadway, its hat fifteen feet away, its arms outflung and half-curled as in death.

Marshal Fogarty was gingerly massaging one set of knuckles with the fingers of the opposite hand as he surveyed the ruin he had caused.

Hugh leaned to flop the rangeboss over onto his back. What little light came from the shop showed a flung-back streak of scarlet on Jess Bell's right cheek with more scarlet trickling from a smashed mouth.

Joe came a little closer, eyed his victim dispassionately, and very calmly said, "Hugh: there's our excuse."

Pepperdine looked perplexed.

"To get Davy to come to town. I'll lock him up and pass the word he was roarin' drunk, an' if someone don't come to pay his fine an' get him out of town, I'm goin' to prefer felony charges an' hold him for the next circuit-ridin' judge that comes along. . . . Lend me a hand gettin' him over my shoulder."

Hugh helped, balancing the inert figure until Fogarty was ready to walk away; then Joe had something else to say. "Damned good thing for you I had to make my final round before turning in. An' I damned near didn't make it, either. See you in the morning."

CHAPTER 17

An Excited Town

McGREGOR'S REACTION TO WHAT HIS OLD FRIEND related to him over breakfast the next morning was typical of his nature. "Everything happens when I'm not around. You been over to the jailhouse yet this morning?"

Pepperdine hadn't. "No. Hurry up an' finish eating."

When they got across the road, the jailhouse door was unlocked, but there was no sign of Marshal Fogarty. As they were standing there, James pointed. Fogarty had just left the saloon and was striding toward Henry Pohl's place. James muttered.

They hiked up to the saloon, where the only customers were three old gaffers from among the tarpaper shacks at the lower end of town playing toothpick poker.

Rusty was wearing one of the elegant brocaded vests he was noted for and smiled genially as McGregor and Pepperdine approached the bar.

Rusty spoke first. "Joe was just in here. He arrested Barber's rangeboss last night drunk as a lord an' bein' troublesome. But like I told him, Bell didn't get drunk in here. He must've had a bottle with him."

Hugh and James exchanged a look, ordered two, tepid beers they did not want, and killed a half hour with Rusty before returning to the roadway.

Dr. Pohl and Marshal Fogarty were standing on the doctor's porch in conversation. Hugh made a guess. "They're talkin' about the sick woman. Maybe she died."

James gave his friend a sour look. "I got to get back to work. If anythin' comes up, let me know. If he don't mention organizin' a reception committee here in town, let me know about that, too, because it's got to be done."

When Hugh entered the harness shop George greeted him with a broad smile. "Is somethin' goin' on in town, Mr. Pepperdine?"

Hugh had his back to the youth while tying his apron as he replied. "Where'd you ever get that idea?"

"I didn't. Mr. Dennis did. He's got a real knack for takin' Sheridan's pulse. He said last night at dinner there was somethin' in the wind."

"Yeah, dust," growled Hugh, turning to survey the items scattered here and there with little scraps of paper tied to them. He selected a Yankee britching that had thread so badly frayed that the layers of leather were parting. As he took it to the worktable he asked George about Hank's daughter, and that was a mistake. Taciturn George Jefferson, the lad who last season didn't say ten words all day long, launched into a eulogy that might have gone on longer than it did if a pair of freshly shorn rangemen hadn't walked in smelling powerfully of the French toilet water the local barber sprinkled liberally at every opportunity. They were young, stalwart, pleasant-faced men who had just delivered fifteen Durham bulls up at Barber's cow camp and had been given a day off to get sheared, shaved, and rested before going to work. One of them removed a frayed old bulletbelt and tossed it atop the counter for Hugh to examine as the rider asked if it could be repaired.

It could. "Take a day or two, but we can pull out the rotted thread and resew it."

"What'll that cost?"

Hugh eyed the cowboys. "You work around here?"

The owner of the belt replied. "For Mr. Barber. We brought up some bulls for him and start work tomorrow."

Hugh reexamined the belt, more meticulously this time because he needed time to think. As he was putting the belt down for the second time he smiled at the riders. "It'll cost a dollar to fix the belt, an' you can

140

come for it any time after tomorrow. By the way, too bad about Mr. Barber's rangeboss."

Both riders looked blank, and one said, "We ain't met him yet. Did he have an accident?"

Hugh's smile was wry as he replied. "I expect you could call it an accident. Last night he was smoked to the gills and raisin' a ruckus around town. Marshal Fogarty put him to sleep then locked him up."

The cowboys stared, muttered a little, and departed. As Hugh was turning away from the counter George spoke to him. "Jess? Jess Bell? Are you sure?"

Hugh was dead sure. No one in town could have been more sure, but his reply indicated otherwise. "That's what I heard. You know him, George?"

"Yes. I rode out with him a few times."

"Nice feller, is he?"

"Well, I wouldn't say that, but he's good with livestock, knows the range up here."

"Not a nice feller, then, eh?"

George stopped working. "Him and Mr. Barber are real close. The joke among the riders was that if Davy told Jess to jump, Jess'd ask how high. He's a bad man to cross. The other riders said he could whip any man his heft in the country."

"You got along with him though?"

"Mostly by stayin' out of his way, an' when we'd go bull hunting or heifer hunting, I didn't ask questions, I just did what he told me to do."

"Real good with his fists, eh?"

"I never saw him get into a fight, but the other men have. They said he was so fast his opponents didn't even see it comin' until he'd knocked them flat."

Hugh was plucking thread from the britching without looking up from what he was doing, but even if he had,

141

and even if George had seen his face, there would have been nothing visible there to indicate amusement. Hugh simply said, "There never was a fightin' man born that there wasn't another fightin' man somewhere who couldn't beat him."

George frowned. "Do you figure he tangled with Marshal Fogarty?"

"Drunks usually do, son, an' if this feller did, then he'll be down there in his cell this morning a lot sorrier than before."

"What'll happen? Drunks don't stay in jail, do they?"

"Oh, yeah they do. Specially if they been troublesome. That's one thing Marshal Fogarty don't overlook."

George stopped working to scowl in the direction of the doorway. "Mr. Barber won't like this. He leans real heavy on his rangeboss."

Hugh's answer to that was quietly given. "All Mr. Barber's got to do is come to town and pay the fine."

George went back to work without comment until he had to pause to make sewing thread and wax it; then he said, "He'll come. Maybe even before those two bull drivers go back to camp. He'll miss Jess before then."

Hugh went right on plucking thread. "That'll be nice," he murmured.

Later in the day, while Hugh was sucking his teeth in front of the cafe after having finished his midday meal, Joe Fogarty came across to get a couple of little tin pails from the cafeman for his prisoner, one with watery stew in it, the other with black coffee. Joe stopped near the harnessmaker and wagged his head. "I didn't hit him that hard. Henry came down this morning because his damned face is puffed up like a flour sack. He's got a busted jaw."

142

Hugh made a little, mildly reproving clucking sound. "Now that's a real shame, isn't it?"

Fogarty looked closely at the older man, then straightened up. Before he could speak Hugh told him about the pair of bull drivers coming to his store, and also about what George'd had to say.

Fogarty was still studying the older man's face when he said, "You sly old goat."

Hugh spread his hands. "You want him in town, don't you?"

The marshal didn't reply; he brushed past to enter the cafe leaving Pepperdine out there still sucking his teeth.

The day passed slowly and uneventfully, although Hugh glanced up from his work, keeping an eye on roadway traffic, until close to sundown. Then the somewhat dull, big young man named Jim Young walked in. He had a tannery at the extreme north end of town where the town council had decreed he had to move a year or so earlier because of complaints about flies and the odor. He was wearing a big smile as he placed a filthy pair of leather traces on the counter. "They're crackin' real bad, Mr. Pepperdine. I'd oil 'em myself, but right now I don't have the time."

George raised his head slowly. The smell couldn't be solely attributable to the filthy traces. Jim smiled at George, who smiled back, looking slightly strained from the effort.

Hugh approached the counter, breathing through his mouth; that way a man couldn't smell anything. He didn't touch the leather; he eyed it though, and wagged his head. "Jim, that leather's as dead as last year's flowers. Oilin' alone won't make it any better." Hugh's eyes lifted to the big younger man's face. "Why did you let them go so long?"

"Well, the rest of the harness ain't crackin', Mr. Pepperdine."

"The rest of the harness don't get dragged through what this part's been through. I'll tell you what; we'll make you a new set for half price."

"You don't have to do that, Mr. Pepperdine. I been doin' real good this summer. I been able to buy green hides dirt cheap. Some of 'em was already beginning to get maggoty by the time they was brought in, but—"

"We'll make you a new set, Jim. Come back in three, four days. All right?"

"I'll sure be obliged to you, Mr. Pepperdine. I got to go eat."

Hugh remained in place at the counter after the tanner had departed. From behind him, George cleared his throat. "I guess they don't use soap to tan hides, do they?"

Hugh was thinking of something else. "That feller who owns the cafe has a fit every time Jim goes down there."

George was twisting thread over his upper leg when he replied. "I can't imagine why."

Hugh took the offensive traces out back and tossed them in the shade, returned, washed his hands, and went back to work. But as brief as this interlude had been, the smell was still strong when Silas Browning's top driver walked in carrying a broken bellyband. He stopped midway and made a grimace. "Whatever you been doin' in here," he said to Hugh, "you'd ought to have done it outside."

Hugh dried his hands on the way to the counter. With one hand he pawed at the torn bellyband, with the other hand he felt for the bottle under the counter and wordlessly set it up. Jack Carpenter smiled as he

144

reached for the bottle. "Damned mule got his foot through that thing, busted it and threw himself in the process." Carpenter swallowed, blew out a lurid breath, and recapped the bottle. "Silas needs it no later'n tomorrow."

Hugh's answer was given while he was fingering the leather. "Silas needs everything tomorrow. Look in that corner; all that work is ahead of his."

Carpenter leaned to look then pulled back with a shrug. "Whenever you can get to it," he said, eyeing the bottle, but Hugh shoved it back out of sight before the driver could raise a hand.

"What's goin' on down in Bordenton?" he asked the driver and got back a casually given but nonetheless startling reply.

"Somebody raided the bank down there. I heard they made off with ten thousand dollars."

Both George and Hugh gazed at the stage driver, but he'd told them all he knew, and as he was departing he winked at Hugh. "If Pete Donner up here in Sheridan hears about that, he'll be out recruitin' gun-guards from all over the countryside."

Just short of sundown Joe Fogarty appeared in the doorway. He already knew about the bank robbery at Bordenton and had taken the only precaution he could take. At the demand of Sheridan's nervous banker, Pete Donner, he had alerted the local vigilantes, who were mostly local merchants and their employees.

Donner had cause for anxiety. His Sheridan Bank and Trust Company had been raided a couple of years earlier, and Pete had the scars to prove it.

Hugh went to supper early, and while he was at the cafe learned that the Bordenton raid was not only common knowledge but was the prime topic of conversation.

When he was up at Morton's saloon after dusk had settled the same situation existed. All the talk was of the raid. It included some grim predictions about what would happen to any outlaws who might appear in Sheridan.

It did not occur to Hugh that everyone capable of using a gun would now have one at his side throughout Sheridan until James McGregor came in, saw Hugh, and joined him at a table, looking harassed. He had barely dropped into a chair before he said, "Hell, you'd think the British was comin' again. I go all year makin' conchos and whatnot, repairin' a few guns, and all of a sudden today I sold seven guns and got eleven to work over." James grimaced. "More business in one day than I've done in ten weeks."

Hugh sat listening thoughtfully. It did not require much imagination to guess what could happen if the outlaws and Davy Barber descended upon Sheridan at the same time. Not just Davy Barber; just anyone at all who wasn't a resident of the town and who would be wearing a weapon. Maybe four or five armed travelers or some cowboys passing through.

McGregor cocked his head. "What are you so quiet about?"

"Just thinkin' about everyone goin' around on a hair trigger and our scheme to get Davy to come to town."

"Where is the connection? Folks know Davy."

"Odds are pretty good, James, that he'll come with his riders. But whether he does or not, when Joe steps up to arrest him—if there's trouble, and my money is on the side that says there will be—the whole town'll boil out to fight after the first gunshot."

McGregor scoffed. "Naw. I just told you, folks know

Davy on sight. Maybe most of 'em got no use for him, but nobody's goin' to think he's goin' to rob the bank."

Hugh sighed. "I sure hope you're right."

"You been workin' too hard," the gunsmith said. "You want a drink? I'll go get us a bottle."

"Not for me, thanks all the same."

McGregor settled back down in his chair. "Me neither."

They were sitting like a pair of mutes when Marshal Fogarty walked in and was immediately engulfed by excited townsmen. Hugh watched for a while then rose. "See you tomorrow, James," he said, and left the noisy saloon to head for his shop and the lean-to out behind it.

CHAPTER 18

Waiting

SOMEONE SAID THAT NO MATTER WHAT KIND OF A crisis arose, and regardless of how ordinary and nondescript human beings were, for every crisis there was a leader who would appear for each occasion.

Hugh had heard that. He hadn't really made up his mind about its validity, but the morning after the news reached town of the Bordenton raid he told possum-bellied Reg Lee, the liveryman-horsetrader, that it had to be the gospel truth, because two-thirds of the menfolk in Sheridan were going around armed to the gills, making suggestions and giving orders.

Lee was standing with his back to the stove gazing out the roadway window. He'd arrived early to get one of a set of nice driving lines skived, joined, and sewn. The lines belonged to Henry Pohl who had let one line

147

fall on the ground where his buggy mare had cut it into two pieces with a toe calk.

Reg had already dispensed with his judgment of anyone who'd use a driving line like that and was now watching the yonder sidewalk with its bonneted ladies carrying net shopping bags and their menfolk going around like the Dalton boys with hardware pulling their britches down.

"An' suppose," he said, out of a clear blue sky, "no outlaws show up? Look at 'em out there. Hey, where's your apprentice?"

"At the cafe havin' breakfast," Hugh stated, taking the torn driving line to the worktable where he skived both ends, squared them, applied a light glue, then went to the sewing horse with them.

Reg hoisted his trousers, which always seemed in imminent peril of falling, watched Hugh sew for a moment, then went to lean on the counter. "There's some kind of trouble goin' on," he mused aloud. "I was up at the emporium yestiddy, and Hank said things ain't normal and ain't been for several days, and that was before all this talk about a raid down at Bordenton."

Hugh concentrated on what he was doing in silence.

Lee shifted until his weight was supported by both feet before speaking again. "Did you know Joe's got Davy Barber's foreman locked up?"

Hugh nodded. "Yeah."

"I heard over at the abstract office the rangeboss insulted some lady here in town, an' got drunk, an' was goin' to hooraw the town."

Hugh sighed. "Nothin' like the imaginations in a cow town, Reg."

"Well, he's got him locked up, ain't he?"

"So they say," Hugh replied as he was approaching

148

the counter. "Here. That'll be two bits, an' next time you see Henry tell him to keep the lines over the front of the dashboard."

Lee hitched his britches, paid up, nodded, and walked out into the sunbright early morning where the gray smoke of breakfast stove fires had flattened out over town to either eventually dissipate or to be blown away if, and when, a breeze arrived. There were very few pleasant days when there wasn't at least a light breeze.

Hugh went to lean in his doorway. Sheridan was a nice town. It had progressed from a log and wattle hide camp to a place with an arrow-straight main thoroughfare running due north and south, lined with structures made of rough but dimensioned lumber with trees on both sides of Main Street and several impressive buildings, including the local bank made of genuine red brick.

Taken as a whole the people were no better and probably no worse than people in other towns of the same size, although there were times when Hugh Pepperdine would not have bet a plugged *centavo* that this was true; but, as he candidly admitted to himself, when a body reaches seventy or thereabouts, it's a little harder to find all the splendid virtues in folks a man'd had no difficulty seeing in them when he was twenty.

North of the gun shop, midway between it and the tannery, Pete Donner from the bank, a dark, stocky, unsmiling individual, was in heated conversation with Joe Fogarty, who not only towered above Donner but who was half-again as broad. Even at that distance Hugh had to smile at the expression on Fogarty's face. It was a mixture of painful forbearance and annoyance.

When they parted, and Donner headed for his brick bank building, Hugh's smile widened. The banker's

149

coat bulged with the unmistakable outline of a shoulder-holstered side arm.

Marshal Fogarty crossed to Henry Pohl's cottage and disappeared inside.

Hugh still did not know whether that woman up there was dead or alive. From what he knew, he thought she had a right to give up the ghost.

The cafeman came padding up the opposite plankwalk carrying one of those net shopping bags as he headed for Dennis's store. He saw Hugh in the doorway and did an uncharacteristic thing: he threw up his arm and waved.

Hugh looked left and right to be sure the wave was meant for him, then waved back. From behind him George said, "It's like the Fourth of July, isn't it?"

Hugh turned. The tall youth, who had filled out to become a big, powerful man in just one year, was tying his apron. The signs of adulthood, while clearly visible—as they would remain for the rest of George's life, perhaps becoming even more visible as the years passed—were at this time still not capable of mitigating the looks and a few of the mannerisms of youth.

Hugh turned back into the shop as he answered the lad's question. "Yeah. More like a shootin' gallery. Everybody's wearin' a gun. Where's yours?"

George eyed Pepperdine's shellbelt-free middle when he replied. "The same place yours is, hangin' up in the back room. I'm a harnessmaker. I don't want to shoot anybody, an' I don't have any money in the bank. . . . That leather the tanner brought in is drawin' flies out back. Maybe I'd better fetch it inside, get the measurements and get to work."

Hugh nodded. He was going to miss the lad. Not just because of the fondness he'd developed for him, but because he would no longer be there to jump right in and work until late. Hugh was going to have to do everything himself as he'd done before George had come along, and he'd gotten to like having a little leisure time.

Maybe that son of a bitch Davy Barber had been right last year without realizing it. Maybe Hugh did need an apprentice.

Two solemn-faced horsemen riding side-by-side passed along from the southern end of town. They were dusty from the trail, tucked-up-hungry looking, and although they seemed to miss nothing from below their tipped-down hat brims, they ignored the people who glanced up and nodded.

Hugh was at his worktable and did not see them. They did not progress as far north as the harness works anyway; they turned in out front of the jailhouse, swung off, and pushed inside. If Hugh had seen this he could have told them Joe was up at the doctor's place.

They emerged from the jailhouse, eyed the town briefly, then made a beeline for the cafe, which still had a few diners, though most of the cafe's customers had eaten long ago and gone to their places of employment.

An hour later, with sunlight as bright as ever but with less warmth to it than there would have been if this was midsummer, the two men parted, one to each side of the roadway as they passed among the business establishments, still seeking the local lawman. When one of them reached McGregor's gun works, his companion entered the harness shop. Hugh looked up, nodded, and began drying his hands in expectation of having a paying customer.

The leathery, unsmiling man looked vaguely familiar to Hugh. When he approached the counter and spoke

Hugh finally placed him. He was one of a pair of partners who owned the drayage company down at Bordenton. His name was Will Long. His partner's name was Charley Hemstreet, but Hugh had no idea Hemstreet was over at McGregor's place as Will Long removed his riding gloves, folded them under and over his shellbelt, and said, "Sheridan looks like it's gettin' ready to have a shootin' match."

Hugh nodded. "Yeah. We heard about your bank gettin' raided yestiddy."

Long leaned on the counter. "News travels fast, don't it? Well, you folks can set back. We caught them before dark last night, an' they wasn't comin' north anyway; they went east."

George stopped working to look up and listen. Hugh was too surprised to speak for a moment, then all he said was, "Is that a fact?" Then he gestured with one arm toward the roadway and laughed. "I don't know whether folks'll be relieved or disappointed. We been bracin' for a raid since we first heard the news."

Will Long smiled back but politely, not enthusiastically. He'd been in the saddle since yesterday afternoon and was tired all the way through. "My partner'n me was two-thirds of the way to Sheridan over eastward when the posse overtook them in a dry wash restin' their animals. The other fellers took 'em back to Bordenton, but me'n my partner figured it was closer to come on into Sheridan to eat, get our horses looked after, and bed down for eight or ten hours."

Will Long was still at the counter when Marshal Fogarty walked in. Hugh gestured. "This here is Mr. Long from Bordenton. He's got the cartage business down there. Him an' his partner."

As Joe nodded and Will Long returned the salute,

Hugh also said, "They run down the bank robbers last night an' by now got 'em locked up down in Bordenton."

Fogarty's brows shot up. Long added a few details to what the harnessmaker had said, then pushed up off the counter. "Is the roominghouse still up at the north end of town on the west side?"

When he was assured that it still was, he nodded and without another word headed doorward with three sets of eyes watching as he left the harness shop.

Joe stared at Hugh, who shrugged on his way back toward the worktable. "Now the blarney will start over at the saloon. All we're goin' to hear for the next day or two is what all the brave citizens of Sheridan would have done if them outlaws had come up here."

Hugh turned, saw the look on Joe Fogarty's face, and his humor faded. "Did she die?"

Fogarty shook his head. "No. She's still alive. In fact, this morning she ate a good breakfast, accordin' to Henry, and wanted to walk around a little. But Henry told me his opinion hasn't changed a bit. She's on borrowed time."

"What's he goin' to do with her? Shouldn't she be sent down to Buttonwillow where her daughter is?"

Joe shoved big hands into trouser pockets and studied the patterns George was working with as he replied. "I offered to pay her fare down there. She said no, and this much I've learned about that lady: When she says no, that's exactly what she means."

Hugh's response was oblique and bone dry. "She should have said no about sixteen years ago, wouldn't you say?"

Fogarty let that pass. "Anyone know where Davy is?"

Hugh would have given a negative reply, but George

spoke first. "Two of his riders was in yesterday. By now they been back at the camp a long time. Plenty of time to tell Mr. Barber where Jess Bell is an' plenty of time for him to make up his mind what he's goin' to do about it."

Fogarty stood wide-legged in thought for a moment then, without another word, turned to depart. Hugh halted him at the doorway. "Might not be a bad idea to keep folks wide-eyed, Joe. They're already armed for a bear hunt."

Fogarty turned, fixed Pepperdine with a scalding stare, then left. Hugh reddened, and as George went back to work, he said, "I don't think he liked you tellin' him how to do his job, Mr. Pepperdine."

Gradually Sheridan got back down to its normal routines as the word passed that there would be no bank robbery, that the raiders had been caught and locked up down at Bordenton.

In time most people were relieved, even the bitterhearted manager of the bank; but James McGregor's relief was not total because he'd seen the possibility of a raid on the Sheridan bank as a complication that would certainly make the arrival of unpredictable Davy Barber and his hard-bitten riding crew a source of considerable confusion.

He hadn't even thought of that until he'd listened to Hugh at the saloon last night, nor did he have time to go over to the harness shop until close to supper time. When he eventually got over there Hugh was alone, cleaning up while examining some work that would be next atop his worktable in the morning, and saw James enter with a casual nod.

"You know about the raiders gettin' caught down yonder?" When McGregor nodded as he walked toward

154

the counter, Hugh also said, "Well, now, we can get back to waitin' for Davy."

McGregor flung out both arms. "Where is he? Sure as hell he knows his foreman's in the *calabozo* by now."

Hugh tossed aside the oily rag he'd been drying his hands with. "He knows by now. Maybe he'll ride in tonight."

But he didn't. The saloon had a full complement of customers, including at least three who watched the clock and listened for horsemen in the roadway: McGregor, Pepperdine, and Joe Fogarty.

Rusty's pale, round face shone with sweat, not from heat because the moment the sun departed there was almost no lingering warmth to the days. He was sweating because business was very brisk. He attributed this to the relief men felt that they hadn't had to turn the town into a battleground.

Fogarty was not drinking. He could not shake free of townsmen for a long time, but when he eventually was able to he approached the distant, dingy table where Pepperdine and McGregor were nursing two little jolt glasses with a bottle in the center of the table. Joe sat down, leaned massive arms atop the scarred wood, and looked from one older man to the other.

"Well," he said, looking longest at Hugh. "That notion of yours to chum him to town—wasn't anythin' wrong with it, except that it didn't work."

Hugh did not dispute this, he simply said, "You ever work cattle this time of year, Joe? They're scattered from hell to breakfast, an' Davy's got thousands of acres to comb over. What I'm gettin' at is that he wouldn't be settin' around no wagon camp this time of the year; he'd be out somewhere an' might not get back for a day or two, maybe longer, maybe not until he's got

155

a big gather to bring back with him."

"You're sayin' he hasn't seen those bull drivers yet?"

"I'm sayin' it's likely that he hasn't," Hugh replied. "But he sure as hell will, an' there's nothin' anyone can do to make that happen any quicker than the good Lord wants it to happen."

CHAPTER 19

Complications and Failures

HUGH WAS CORRECT. NEITHER DAVY NOR ANY OF HIS riders appeared in Sheridan the following day but something else took up a little of the slack. The woman named Harriet Blake, who just about everyone in town believed was Davy Barber's wife, appeared in the Pohl's parlor late in the afternoon with hotly bright eyes and a very healthy high color in her cheeks. She startled Henry by saying she thought she had better return to her lodgings at the roominghouse.

Dr. Pohl's wife was not at home when this event took place, otherwise Henry would have relied on Eleanor's sweetness and tact to dissuade Harriet Blake. He made the effort, but the moment he got close to her all his training and acquired skill as a physician became unnecessary. His nose told him that the woman had been drinking.

How she had managed to locate the whiskey was a mystery but certainly not an unsolvable one since there were several bottles around the cottage. But for Henry, who had treated men in every degree of insobriety but precious few women in that state, the dilemma was compounded by what he knew was a very unpredictable heartbeat.

He adopted an attitude of agreement, which was something else he'd learned over the years when dealing with patients who could be troublesome. He agreed with her while, simultaneously pointing out that it was late in the day, Eleanor would be back from the store shortly with groceries for a three-person meal, and rather than disappoint his wife, it would be better if the woman put off her departure until the following day.

Harriet Blake agreed, wandered around the parlor, paused before a fading picture of a man and a woman in clothes from an earlier time, lifted the heavy, sterling frame to took more closely, and Henry held his breath because the small revolver that had been removed from her purse was lying back there.

Evidently she did not notice the gun when she put the picture down and turned with a nice smile to say how much she owed Henry and his wife. As soon as she could get some money that belonged to her—and which Davy Barber had taken—she would make full restitution.

Henry's relief was palpable. When his wife returned he took her into the operating room and gave her every detail of what had transpired. Eleanor went at once to the kitchen to begin supper and looked into the little room where Harriet Blake was flat out on the bed, sleeping like a log.

The next morning at breakfast time, Eleanor asked her husband to explain just exactly why he did not want her to move back to the hotel.

Henry's explanation was brief and uncomplicated. "She's gaining strength. She needs quiet surroundings to gain more."

"Where did she get the whiskey, Henry?"

He had no idea. "Somewhere. Maybe in the kitchen cupboard, maybe in the surgery room. I don't know. But she gets around very well."

"And she could move back to the hotel, couldn't she?"

He had to agree. "Yes. But Eleanor, she's only been on the mend for a few days. Her heartbeat is still erratic."

"Whiskey won't help that, Henry."

"Maybe not, but I wouldn't take an oath to that. Whiskey's a valuable medicine."

Eleanor gave a wintery smile. "For someone with a bad heart?"

"Possibly."

"When can she move out, Henry?"

"In a few days."

"Three days?"

"Well, all right: three days. Eleanor, you don't like her?"

"Henry, you've said it a hundred times: When everything we can do for people has been done . . ."

He nodded. "Three days. How long before supper?"

"An hour."

"I'm going down to Fogarty's office."

She pecked him on the cheek and turned back to her stove.

Evening was flower-scented, mostly from around town but also from the miles of more distant countryside. Henry saw McGregor locking his front door for the night. Farther along he saw Hank Dennis standing beneath the overhang out front of his store talking to George Jefferson. Marshal Fogarty was not in the jailhouse, which was annoying because Henry wanted to examine the prisoner with the broken jaw.

While he was standing in thick shadows out front of the jailhouse the silhouette of a mounted man approached from the lower end of town; otherwise there was no roadway traffic and almost no pedestrian traffic.

The horseman angled in toward the plankwalk between the jailhouse and its hitchrack, leaned from the saddle to peer at Henry, and straightened up with a disgusted grunt.

"Hello, Doctor. Where's Joe Fogarty?"

Henry answered shortly. "He's not in the jailhouse, Mr. Barber. I don't know where he is."

For a moment the horseman continued to sit in the saddle. He looked from Henry Pohl to the front wall of the jailhouse then, with both gloved hands resting atop the saddlehorn, swung his head to look elsewhere.

Finally he dismounted, led his animal around to the street side of the rack, carelessly looped the reins, and strode over where Henry was standing, tugging off his gloves as he did so. He turned in beside the physician and studied the lighted, fogged-up cafe window that was diagonally opposite the jailhouse. "Maybe havin' supper," he said quietly, as though thinking out loud.

Henry agreed. "Maybe."

The cowman turned, gazed speculatively at the medical practicioner for a moment, then smiled as he spoke. "By any chance have you seen my rangeboss? I know he's locked up in there, but someone said he got hurt too."

Henry had indeed seen Davy Barber's rangeboss. "He has a broken jaw, Mr. Barber."

The stockman's smile died. He stared at the doctor for a long moment before speaking again. "Doctor, when you was treatin' Jess, did he smell of liquor to you?"

159

"No, he didn't. But I heard—"

"Doctor, I can guess what you heard. I heard somethin' about him gettin' drunk and hoorawing the town. I'll tell you somethin' interestin' about Jess Bell, Doctor. He don't drink." At Henry's look of surprise Barber nodded his head in emphasis. "Only genuine cowman I ever run across that didn't drink. At least now an' then."

Henry pondered. He had seen Barber's rangeboss enter the saloon in the company of other stockmen. He also had heard that contradicting Davy Barber was not a wise thing to do, so he said, "Not even once in a while?"

"No sir. Not even once in a while."

At Henry's look Barber's smile returned but without a shred of humor to it. "But Jess is mortal like all the rest of us, so I taken time off to come down to Sheridan and find out just what the hell really happened. I figured maybe Jess broke his habit an' had a drink. Maybe more'n one drink, an' I figured that if he did that, him not being a drinkin' man an' all, why he just might have gone wild and got himself jugged. But you didn't smell liquor on him, so I guess he didn't go hog-wild, did he?"

Henry was uncomfortable. He was also at a loss for words until Barber spoke again.

"Who busted his jaw, Doctor?"

Henry's discomfort was increasing by the second. "I'm a medical man, Mr. Barber. That's my profession, and I very rarely ever go beyond doing my job."

Davy Barber's cold smile vanished as he stood in the darkness regarding the medical man. "In other words, you know who busted his jaw and won't tell me."

Henry saw a large man emerge from the saloon up the opposite roadway. "There's Marshal Fogarty. You

160

should talk to him."

Barber turned, watched the big, dark shape cross the road in the direction of the harness shop where three lamps were burning, and blew out a ragged, big breath. "It'll be him that busted Jess's jaw. Well, maybe you're right, Doctor. Maybe I'd better talk to him."

Henry nodded and smiled as he turned to walk briskly toward the lower end of town for no reason except that prudence dictated a direction as far from the possibility of bad trouble as he could get.

He was passing the lower extent of the public corrals, which adjoined Reg Lee's private network of corrals, when Davy Barber loped past, also heading out of town at the southern end. He did not look over at Henry Pohl, and until Henry was down near the carriage lamplight on the front of Lee's barn, he did not stop walking.

Reg came ambling out chewing a toothpick, saw the doctor, and stopped. After a moment he said, "I got that busted buggy line of yours patched. You owe me four bits."

That was twice what Hugh had charged him, but Reg was not in business for his health. As Dr. Pohl fished out some silver and dropped one medium-sized coin in the liveryman's hand, Lee passed along Pepperdine's admonition. "If you'll keep the lines over the top of the dashboard, they won't get trampled."

Henry nodded. "I'll remember that," he said, and turned abruptly to retrace his steps up as far as the jailhouse, which was still dark, and continued all the way up to the harness works.

When he entered Joe and Hugh were having a cup of coffee at the counter, relaxed and comfortable until Hugh saw the doctor's face. Then he stiffened and asked a question. "The lady upped and died, Henry?"

161

"No." He looked squarely at Marshal Fogarty. "Did you know Barber's rangeboss doesn't drink?"

Both the other men stared until Joe's thick brows began to settle into a puzzled frown. "No, an' if that's got some meanin', Henry, I don't understand it."

"I was standing in front of your office, Joe, not thirty minutes ago when Davy Barber rode up from the south. It was too dark for either of us to recognize the other until he leaned from the saddle to ask where you were. We talked for a few minutes, and that's when he told me his rangeboss doesn't drink. Not even once in a while. He said Bell's about the only cattleman he ever knew who didn't drink, not even a little."

Fogarty's scowl lingered. "He knew Jess's jaw was busted?"

"I told him it was. That was before he told me Bell doesn't drink."

"Then what?"

"I saw you leaving the saloon and told him if he wanted to talk to someone who knew how his rangeboss got hurt, you were crossing the road up yonder. He watched you come in here, said something about maybe he should talk to you, and that's when I walked away."

Fogarty and Pepperdine exchanged a look as Hugh said, "He didn't come up here, Henry."

Pohl knew that. "No, I was down near Lee's barn when he rode past on his way out of Sheridan at the lower end."

For a while nothing more was said. Not until Hugh saw Henry Pohl looking for something to sink down upon and brought forth the undercounter bottle and shoved it at him. "Two swallows will put the starch back in your legs."

Dr. Pohl took the two swallows, handed back the

162

bottle, and still looked like he would like to sit down. Hugh and Marshal Fogarty forgot about him as one of them said, "Well, so much for the trap."

Henry walked out of the shop heading for home. Neither of the other men even looked around as he departed. Hugh considered the bottle, wagged his head at it, and pushed it closer to the marshal, but Fogarty was not in the mood either. Hugh capped it and shoved it back out of sight as the lawman spoke. "He didn't ride away like that because he was afraid to come here an' brace me."

Hugh nodded while groping for his clasp knife and plug.

Fogarty lifted his hat, vigorously scratched, and lowered the hat. "Now it's goin' to be a different horse race, Hugh. He's either goin' to sit up there with maybe someone put out to watch for trouble or he's goin' to get his men together and come down here. Either way, now it's his move."

Hugh got his cud into place, pocketed the knife, and leaned down to stare at the little iron stove with the dented old coffeepot atop it. He thought Joe was probably right but, having had a very recent and unnerving encounter with one of Barber's men right here in his shop, he was inclined to wonder if Barber might not consider a third alternative.

"How about sneakin' into town at night the way Jess Bell caught me plumb off guard?"

Fogarty did not think so. "He's a direct man, Hugh. Ever since I've been in Sheridan an' he's been bringin' up his cattle, if there's one thing I've noticed about Davy Barber, it's that he don't pussyfoot."

Fogarty slapped the countertop as he straightened up. "I wish to hell I could have been down there when he stopped out front."

Pepperdine's reply to that was succinct. "Yeah. If wishes were worth a damn I'd have been the richest man in the world thirty years ago."

Fogarty nodded absently and walked out into the night, leaving Hugh in place at the counter. He was still there fifteen minutes later staring at the stove and coffeepot when George appeared looking mildly uncomfortable. As Hugh's head came around the younger man smiled at him. "We got the date set, Mr. Pepperdine. A week from now at the church. It would have been sooner, but Charlotte's maw said she can't get all the arrangements made in less than a week."

Hugh straightened up, studying the handsome, slightly self-conscious smile of his apprentice. "A week," he murmured. "I expect she can't get everything ready before then for a fact. Well, son, you got my blessing, now I think we'd better turn in. This has been an interestin' day. Good night."

CHAPTER 20

Indignant Old Gaffers

"INTERESTING DAYS" WERE BECOMING ROUTINE, NOT only in town but elsewhere. Buster Henning straddling his new Pepperdine saddle appeared in Sheridan the following morning and threw a wave at Hugh as he walked his horse in the direction of the general store. Hugh watched him tie up down there and go clanking inside, spur rowels rattling across the plankwalk.

George returned from breakfast to announce that Mr. Donner from the bank had been at the cafe, too. When

164

Hugh raised his eyebrows inquiringly, George gave a little snort of a laugh and went after his apron as he said, "I hardly know him, but from the sour look on his face, I'm not sure I've missed very much."

George was working on the tanner's harness while Hugh was scowling over a torn seating leather on a rangeman's rig when Joe Fogarty appeared in the doorway to say, "Good morning. When you got a minute, Hugh, I'll be down at the jailhouse."

George cocked an eye after the marshal had departed. "That don't sound good, Mr. Pepperdine."

Hugh was pitching his apron across the saddle with the torn seating leather when he replied. "Most likely just talk. Joe's good at that." From the doorway he looked back, winked, then proceeded southward with early-morning chill in an otherwise magnificent sunbathed new day.

The town was beginning to look and sound busy. A huge, old battered freight wagon was parked out in front of the smithy where two burly, bearded unkempt-looking men were in deep conversation with the blacksmith about a bowed axle. From across the road Hugh could see the bow without even having to lean down very much. He thought the freighter must have tried to straddle a boulder and had misjudged its size. The only remedy was to block up the big wagon, remove the wheels and axle, see if it couldn't be straightened at the forge, and if not then have a new axle sent from maybe Denver or Chicago, which meant the big wagon would be parked in front of the smithy, possibly for a week or two. That, Hugh knew for a fact, those unwashed, unshaven freighters would be very unhappy about. Not only wouldn't the wagon be able to haul freight, which was how they made their living, but the animals that pulled the wagon, maybe ten or so mules or big horses, would stand around eating their heads off.

As he turned in at the jailhouse he saw one of the bearded freighters throw up both arms, then turn and go stamping away.

Joe Fogarty was sitting at his littered old table with a cup of java, and hefty Buster Henning was wedged into a chair, along the front wall, also holding a cup of coffee. At Hugh's appearance Henning struggled up out of the chair as he nodded, put the cup aside, and smiled at Pepperdine. "See you gents later," he said, and walked back out into the roadway.

Joe pointed to a chair. Hugh sat down, eyed the larger and younger man, and waited.

Fogarty sighed. "It's Davy again. He's not makin' any effort to keep his cattle off Buster's grass, an' one of his cowboys bearded Buster's choreboy, a kid of about fifteen, when they met out a few miles and told him if he tried to turn back any Barber critters the cowboy'd yank him out'n the saddle an' stamp the waddin' out of him."

Hugh looked unperturbed but interested. "Well, like we talked about last night, Davy's trouble. But a ruckus between those two don't have anythin' to do with me."

Joe leaned in. "You said somethin' about if I went out there across that open range with a posse they'd see me comin' an' get ready."

Hugh acknowledged that he'd said something like that, then began to frown faintly as he regarded Fogarty's unwavering stare. "Joe, I got a business to run."

Fogarty neither denied this nor acted as though he had heard what Pepperdine had said. He clasped big hands

166

atop the table and spoke quietly, "I know you used to scout, somethin' like thirty years ago."

"More like twenty years," Hugh said.

"Twenty years ago. You said it last night, Hugh. Specially after he rode into town in the dark last night to reconnoiter. With a whole pocketful of warrants I'd never get close enough to nail him."

"Joe . . . !"

"Let me finish."

"But hell, Joe, that's all open country."

"You never snuck up on any game in open country, Hugh?"

"Sure. An' not just game, but that's before my joints got a little stiff, and I could slither with the best of 'em."

Marshal Fogarty leaned back off the table. "Hugh, there is you'n me an' James McGregor who know what all this is about. You said yourself it can't go any farther or your apprentice's chances here in Sheridan will be ruined."

Pepperdine was scowling fully now as he regarded the younger man. It irritated the hell out of him that Joe Fogarty would bring George into it just to convince Hugh he had an obligation to scout up Davy's cow camp. He would have got up off the chair, but Marshal Fogarty had another two-bits worth to add to what he'd already said, "You can scout him up tonight, in darkness, while I'm gettin' things organized here in town."

Hugh groaned. The last time he and McGregor had ridden out with the town marshal they came back shrunk down to nubbins, tired clean to the marrow in their bones, and adamantly swearing they would never get involved with him again. This sort of thing was for young men.

167

As though Fogarty had read Pepperdine's mind, he said, "There's no one around much any more who can scout up an' stalk, Hugh. I'll have a posse ready to ride by the time you get back in the morning." Fogarty smiled a wheedling smile. "Partner, I need you. The lad needs you, too. So does that sick lady up at Henry's place, an' remember her daughter down in Buttonwillow beaten to a fare-thee-well and maybe injured in other ways that she'll never get over."

Hugh stood up angry and indignant. "Joe, you're goin' to be the death of me one of these days."

Fogarty arose behind his table. "No. All I want to know is whether he's got his crew at the wagon an' if he's there with 'em. If he is, we're not goin' out there. If he's out somewhere on the range, we'll scatter and try'n stalk him. I don't want him dead, an' I sure as hell don't want anyone from town dead, but as far as I'm concerned, Hugh, that son of a bitch is at the end of his rope."

Hugh could at least agree with Joe's last statement. In fact, if it had been left to him he would have yanked all the slack out of Davy Barber's rope long ago. From the jailhouse doorway he said, "Joe, this is positively the last time. We got to agree on that."

Fogarty did not hesitate. "Absolutely the last time, Hugh, and I'm real obliged to you. . . . Tonight?"

"Yes."

"I'll be waitin' in town when you show up tomorrow morning."

That was the agreement. It was sealed with a nod from the big man behind the table and the tall, sinewy older man in the doorway. But this kind of a game always had one additional player—Fate—and it had already been decided that Hugh would not arrive back

168

in Sheridan tomorrow morning.

Instead of returning to the shop, Hugh stamped past Rusty Morton's saloon up to the gun works and stamped inside. James looked up from his gun vise, reached for a rag to wipe his hands on, and said, "You look like someone stole your horse."

Hugh didn't own a horse. He leaned on the counter, speared McGregor with a sulphurous glare, and told him the whole story. As he was finishing, McGregor tossed the oily rag aside, perched on a stool, and spoke very bluntly. "The last time he dragooned us you said that was the last time. We got shot at, damn near died of thirst, lost weight, rode our behinds raw, and come back lookin' like we'd been pulled through a knothole. What's the matter with you anyway?"

"He mentioned that sick woman an' the young girl being put back together down in Buttonwillow. And George."

McGregor was stuffing shag into his evil little pipe as he listened, but he did not speak until he'd puffed up a bluish cloud of fragrant smoke. "You can't scout 'em up in the night by yourself, Hugh."

For a brief moment Pepperdine was poised to release more anger but only for a moment. He leaned on the counter looking steadily at McGregor while he digested the implication, then he rolled his eyes. "This isn't for old men, James." He paused with narrowed eyes, watching color flood into McGregor's face.

It worked every time and it was working now. McGregor snatched the pipe from his mouth. "Old men? An' what are you? You're older'n I am. Besides, your joints give you trouble an' your eyesight—"

"Wait a minute, James. Wait a damned minute. I can see better'n you could thirty years ago. As for my

169

joints—"

"You're crazy, Hugh Pepperdine. I always figured it was likely, and this mornin' I got livin' proof standing on the other side of my damned counter. Crazier'n a pet 'coon. You can't any more scout up Barber by yourself than you can fly!"

"Is that so? An' what good would you be out there, you old haggis eater!"

McGregor jumped off the stool and put his pipe aside as he balled up scarred fists. "Old haggis eater! If you wasn't a friend, Hugh, I'd come around that counter and bore a hole in your belly they could drive a wagon through!"

Hugh felt better than he'd felt since getting out of bed this morning. He said, "You just have supper this evenin', go to bed, an' rest your rickety carcass and sleep well while I get a horse from Reg Lee and ride out as soon as it's good an' dark."

Hugh walked out of the gun shop with a spring in his step. He made it all the way over to the harness works with the same bouncy stride. When he entered and his apprentice looked up, Hugh said, "Son, I got a little errand to run tonight, but I'll be back in the morning. You sort of keep an eye on things, eh?"

George nodded and went back to work. One of the first lessons he had learned was not to ask personal questions. But even if he hadn't learned that lesson, Hugh's attitude implied that whatever the errand was, it didn't amount to much. Besides, George hadn't really been able to concentrate on much beside the fact that by this time next week he'd be a married man.

Later, just after midday, Marshal Fogarty appeared in the doorway to exchange a long look with the harnessmaker. Fogarty nodded very faintly and winked.

Hugh did the same, Fogarty walked away and Hugh went back to work.

Jim Young came in with flies in his wake for the new tugs. George got them for him and placed them flat out on the counter as the big, smiling, not-quite-bright tanner ran an appreciative but very soiled hand gently over them. He looked up at George. "Did you make them?"

George nodded while breathing through his mouth.

"They're downright beautiful. I'd hang 'em on the wall in my shack for decorations if I didn't need to use 'em real bad. How much?"

Hugh replied from the middle distance. "Dollar each. Is that all right?"

The tanner's big face with its coarse features creased into a protesting expression. "Mr. Browning said you'd charge seven dollars."

Hugh smiled. "Did he now? Well, so much for Mr. Browning knowin' what he's talkin' about. Two dollars, Jim, and do us a favor; before they get as bad off as the other set was, bring 'em back so's we can clean 'em and give 'em a coating of oil."

Jim Young placed two silver cartwheels on the counter, picked up his traces, eased them over a shoulder, and with a broad smile and a wave walked back out into the sunshine.

George said, "In a cow camp they'd gang up, haul him to a creek, and scrub him until he was as pink as a baby."

"Except that they'd never hire him on a ranch," stated Hugh. "He don't have the coordination to rope, to move fast, nor to think on his feet. I'd guess Jim's right where he's goin' to be until the day he turns up his toes."

George was back working when he said, "He'll never

get a wife unless he changes a hell of a lot. Don't he know how bad he smells?"

"Used to it," Hugh replied, and let the subject die between them.

Late in the afternoon Rusty Morton appeared out front of his saloon in one of his elaborate and expensive brocaded vests. Hugh admired him through the window. He did not believe he'd seen that particular vest before. Behind him George said, "Charlotte's mother said he's got a dozen of them, an' they cost a lot of money."

"Did she?"

"An' that's his way of compensatin' for not bein' able to catch a wife: gets all preened-up like a peacock to attract a woman."

The back of Hugh's neck reddened. "Well, now, did she tell you Rusty was married once?"

"No. I don't think she knows that."

Hugh dared not pursue this conversation so he went back to work. Somewhere down the road, maybe soon and more likely later, George was going to get to know his mother-in-law. George was no one's fool. But Hugh would have let himself be dragged behind wild horses before he would put even a legitimate cloud on the lad's rosy horizon.

McGregor put his face in the doorway and glared, did not say a word, and walked away. George threw Hugh a quizzical look, and Hugh laughed and shook his head without saying anything.

The sun sank, shadows formed. Hugh and George went down to the cafe for supper and returned to the shop where Hugh worked until dusk was settling, then hung up his apron and went to his back room. When he was ready he left by an alley door and walked through gathering darkness toward the southern end of town.

Sheridan was winding down; the blacksmith who had been working at his anvil had quit for the day, that big old freight wagon nearly obscuring the front of his shop. It was propped up on big, wooden blocks.

Men were appearing heading for the cafe. Fogarty's jailhouse door was open, but there was no sign of Joe. Hugh speculated briefly about Jess Bell in there eating stew and drinking black coffee with his face swollen to half the size of a watermelon. If Bell never remembered anything else in his old age, providing he had an old age, he sure as hell would remember the town of Sheridan and its lawman who had fists as big and hard as rocks.

Reg Lee's nightman was standing on a chair midway up the runway to light a lamp. As Hugh turned, a voice as dry as old corn husks spoke from the shadows. "Well, hell, it's about time. I figured you was maybe goin' to weasel out, an' I'd have to go up there myself."

Hugh looked into the shadows. "Instead of standin' around here waitin' you could have had 'em rig out two horses, James."

McGregor snorted. "You blind? What's that look like tied up front?"

CHAPTER 21

"Tomorrow is Sunday."

IT WAS A PLEASANT EVENING WITH A SHARD OF A MOON and a vast panoply of stars. By the time they got within a couple of miles of their destination McGregor's derogatory comments about Pepperdine's old hogleg six-gun had ended. They spoke occasionally, mostly

173

about what might lie ahead. Hugh, who had no booted carbine and rode with both hands belt-buckle high, wrinkled his nose. "They been gathering," he mused softly.

McGregor nodded. He'd detected the scent of cattle some time back. "Kind of early though."

Hugh disagreed. "Not if you got a lot of first-calf heifers."

McGregor let the topic die. He was not as knowledgeable as his companion about cattle.

Hugh resurrected the subject. "They got a habit of gettin' hung up with their first calves. Ten mile out on the range, they die. If you got 'em close where you can watch 'em, ride through 'em every day or two, you can wait until they go down from strainin', sneak up, put a rope around the little legs, and pull 'em. Sometimes, if they're backwards, you got to roll up your sleeves, reach in, turn the little critter around, an' then pull it out."

McGregor was not listening; he was peering into the gloom. In the distance he could see cattle in their beds. As he and Pepperdine got closer, the cattle sprang up, very watchful, unwilling to flee unless the horsemen got close.

A big Durham bull walked forward and halted to challenge the horsemen. Unlike Davy Barber's razorback cattle, the Durhams didn't have horns worth a damn, but they had heft that could be just as bad if they caught a mounted man during a charge.

Hugh ignored the big bull. When James eased slightly to one side Hugh said, "It's not him you got to watch out for. If there's calves with those cows you better watch the cows. When they got babies they'll charge a railroad engine. All he's goin' to do, unless we crowd

174

him, is stand there pawin' dirt."

They angled clear of the birthing ground and did not stop until Hugh held up a hand. He'd detected the smell of wood smoke.

The land on all sides was flat to gently rolling. It had hummocks of stout buffalo grass and a few trees but not down where McGregor and Pepperdine were sitting in their saddles, trying to locate the position of the wagon camp.

McGregor grumbled. "A little more light would help."

Hugh did not comment; he swung from the saddle and stood at the head of his horse. He did not want to get too close, otherwise Barber's remuda would pick up the scent of strange horses and get restless. Hugh looked at his partner and grinned. "Like old times, James."

McGregor scowled. "Not for me it isn't. Can you see anythin' up there?"

Hugh couldn't, nor had he been looking for the camp. He led off to their left, where a patch of starlight was obscured by a bosquet of trees. Over there, after they had tied their animals, Hugh said, "Try to skyline the wagon."

They paced ahead, occasionally halting to look and listen. When Hugh got flat down and squinted against the northward sky he looked at James and smiled. As he rose he pointed. McGregor had to squat before he saw it—the round top of an old camp wagon whose patched, soiled canvas over ash bows did as that bosque of tree had done; it blocked out the stars.

McGregor straightened up, gripping the saddlegun he'd brought from town. He leaned and whispered. "There'll be a nighthawk around here somewhere."

Hugh shrugged and moved forward again but slowly

175

and very carefully this time. The only comment he made was to the effect that it was a good thing they were sneaking up on cowmen rather than sheepmen. Sheepmen always had dogs with them.

McGregor sucked in a breath and grabbed his companion's arm. A tiny red light had flared and dimmed no more than three hundred feet ahead of them to the right.

Hugh had seen the cigarette's glow, too. They knelt in the grass to skyline the man, but he was standing on the near side of his horse. They could skyline the horse very well, but discerning the nighthawk was more difficult. It did not matter very much. Hugh brushed McGregor with his fingers and turned back as they soundlessly retreated a fair distance. They then went ahead again but far enough not to be detected by the nighthawk and more westerly.

This time, with the chill increasing as the night advanced, they got to within a hundred yards of the camp and halted to again sink to one knee. When James leaned to whisper, Hugh glared him into absolute silence.

Davy Barber's old wagon, with its tongue on the ground, had been positioned so that it formed the east side of a rope corral. The horses over there were awake but watchful rather than excited. One man-smell to a horse was the same as another man-smell. Whether they, could differentiate was improbable, but whether they could or not, to a range animal man-smell simply meant two-legged creatures, nothing more.

A pair of strange horses would have got a different reaction, but the strange horses were downcountry, out of scenting distance.

Hugh leaned with both arms crossed over one leg as

he studied the camp. There was a very faint glow of coals from the supper fire, and moonlight was minimal, so it required a fairly long stretch of time for him to locate and count the number of lumpy bedrolls scattered at random.

McGregor was as still as stone. Somewhere over near the wagon, perhaps beneath it—a favorite place for rangemen to bed down—a man coughed, cleared his pipes with considerable force, and spat. That one, at least, was not asleep.

Hugh concentrated on that area. He saw a man roll up to his feet, stamp into his boots, and raise both arms in a mighty stretch. Then he turned, heading directly for the place where Pepperdine and McGregor were watching.

McGregor stiffened. Hugh felt him do it but did not take his eyes off the approaching rangeman. If they turned to scuttle away, and, assuming they managed that without making a noise (which was improbable as the night was utterly still and silent), the rangeman would certainly be able to make them out once they started moving.

Hugh leaned to whisper faintly, "Get belly-down but don't move."

McGregor obeyed, pushed his carbine ahead a little, and held it in both hands. He scarcely breathed as the rangerider loomed above them a fair distance eastward.

Hugh was pressing into the ground as the rangeman stopped, yawned mightily, then moved around a tangle of harness and saddlery on a slightly divergent course. He went out a couple of hundred feet and stopped again, examining the sky. The men flat in the grass heard water running.

McGregor's head sank to the ground. Hugh did not once look away, not even after the cowboy stamped his feet a couple of times before turning back in the direction of the distant wagon.

He leaned to touch McGregor and jerked his head. They had seen what they'd come out here to ascertain. It was now time to withdraw.

They were moving out and around the area where they'd seen the nighthawk when a calving heifer in a hideaway thicket sprang up with a bawl and charged.

On a still, utterly silent late night the noise she made was loud enough to awaken the dead. As Hugh and McGregor parted in flight the cow appeared, with her mouth open. She had detected the man-smell first. After she broke out of the brush patch she still could not see the fleeing men, but scent was no longer as important to her as sound, and they were making enough of it for her to go after the man nearest to her, which was Hugh Pepperdine.

He'd been caught like this several times in his lifetime, knew exactly what would happen if the cow overtook him. He ran faster than he'd run in twenty years with the cow grunting and bawling as she closed the distance between them.

McGregor, off to Hugh's left, out of sight in the night, slackened off a little as he listened to the cow moving in a different direction. He was beginning to feel relief when another sound reached him. A mounted man was loping from the east, probably that nighthawk coming to investigate the noise. If he thought it was a wolf the cow was chasing, he'd be riding with a gun in his fist.

McGregor hesitated long enough for the rider to pass by northward somewhere, then James also turned in that direction. Elsewhere the noise and turmoil had roused Barber and his riding crew, but though they rose up in

178

their soogans to listen, none of them crawled out.

Hugh did not hear the rider; he was frantically looking for a tree, a jumble of rocks, anything he could use to prevent the cow from reaching him. What he eventually found was not what he'd been seeking. He was sucking air like a fish out of water, looking back instead of forward, when the ground abruptly dropped away in front of him. He fell hard, went end over end until he was near the bottom of the arroyo and fetched up in a flourishing stand of thorny buck-brush.

The cow was out of breath but still on the prod as she hurled dirt in a slamming halt atop the abrupt drop-off, swinging her head from side to side, tongue lolling, saliva dripping from the corners of her mouth.

Hugh burrowed into the underbrush, ignoring rips in his shirt and scratches on his arms and face until he was in so far he felt safe.

What he thought was sweat turned out to be blood from a number of gouges in his flesh. As he jockeyed around into a sitting position he said, "Joe Fogarty, I'm goin' to break half the danged bones in your carcass." He shifted his weight a little, hoping to be able to see out, when a pain like fire ran up his right leg. He had to lock his jaws even as he felt for the hip holster to see if his gun had broken loose from its tiedown. It hadn't, but the pain in his right leg continued unabated.

He did not see the cow up there, did not spend more than a moment looking for her, and was gingerly exploring the injured leg, when he heard a mounted man to the east somewhere. The rider rolled out a series of searing curses as the fighting cow turned on him. He shook out the turk's-head end of his lariat and expertly stung the cow's face several times before she would turn back. He was so angry with the cow, he did not

179

even look down the arroyo as he pushed the cow back toward camp.

Hugh settled back against spiky underbrush, sucking air into a pair of lungs that seemed to be on fire. As long as he didn't move the leg the pain was minimal. He looked at the sky, breathed hard, and felt like swearing at the top of his voice. When some of the agitation had subsided he began to worry about James McGregor. He also began worrying about his situation; maybe Barber's riders wouldn't find him in the thorny patch, most likely they wouldn't, but just how in the holy hell was he ever going to get back to Sheridan!

He had no idea that McGregor was trying to track him by following the deep-scored imprints the angry cow had made. It was not a difficult undertaking, moon or no moon. That old girl had been digging in with every jump as she tried to locate the two-legged creature she'd been convinced had been sneaking up to get her baby calf.

McGregor heard the rider. He even sank in the grass to watch the man whipping the cow in his anger. McGregor reached the lip of the fateful arroyo and sank to one knee, studying churned earth. He was no tracker and had never professed to be. But he didn't have to be as long as he could trace out cow tracks in churned earth, and eventually the shod-horse tracks of that furious nighthawk, too.

McGregor's difficulty arose as he squatted on the lip of the arroyo with nothing further to see or feel. He sat until the commotion back at the wagon camp had subsided as disgruntled rangemen crawled back down inside their soogans. He was ready to believe Pepperdine had escaped the cow and was probably on his way back to the place where they'd left their horses when something dark and shapeless down the near side of the gully caught and held his attention. It could have been a nocturnal animal, except that it did not move.

McGregor stood up, looked in all directions, and cocked his head to listen before starting down the slope toward the dark object.

It was Pepperdine's hat!

McGregor stood holding it in one hand as he tried to imagine where the man might be who had run out from under it. To someone with tracking savvy the answer would have been obvious; to James McGregor it was not. Nevertheless, he continued on down into the arroyo, moving slowly and as quietly as possible.

When he was within thirty feet of a dense thicket of thorny underbrush he thought he heard a small animal close by and stood motionless, listening. It wasn't an animal; it was a man's groan.

Using the saddlegun to push underbrush aside, McGregor penetrated the thicket and stopped stone-still as someone, out of sight but not very distant, cocked a handgun.

McGregor barely moved his lips. "Hugh? Is that you?"

The answer came after a moment of hesitation. "Yeah. I busted my leg."

McGregor pushed on through, leaned the Winchester aside, looked at his old friend's drawn face, and dropped the hat as he knelt to look at the injured leg. He had barely touched it when Pepperdine said, "The ankle. I must have fallen on it when I tumbled off that high place before rollin' down here. Where is that damned cow?"

"Gone. A rider got her turned back. Grit your teeth; I got to pull the boot off."

Hugh not only gritted them, he ground them as spirals of excruciating agony shot up from his lower leg. It did not abate even after the boot was off and McGregor was leaning down to gently feel the swelling. When he sat back he shook his head. Their saddle stock was close to a mile southward. In his prime he might have been able to carry Pepperdine that far, but not now.

Hugh did not wait for the gunsmith's assessment; he gestured with one arm. "Go on. Take my horse back with you. There isn't no other way, James."

"I don't like leavin' you here."

"They won't find me. For all they'll know in the mornin' it was a wolf caused the ruckus. Take my horse back with you an' tell Fogarty ol' Davy's got his whole riding crew down here at his camp, an' as near as I could make out, there's eight men countin' Davy."

McGregor handed Pepperdine his old hat and waited until it was in place before speaking again. "How in hell can we get you out of here without Davy knowin' we came for you? It's got to be done with a wagon, Hugh."

"Maybe tomorrow night, James. It'll be Saturday and his men'll want to ride in to let off steam."

McGregor shook his head. "Today is Saturday, Hugh. Tomorrow is Sunday."

"It can't be, dammit. They was all in camp this evening."

McGregor was undeterred. "Maybe he told 'em to stay around. But one thing I know as well as I know my name. Tomorrow is Sunday."

CHAPTER 22

"Hell Yes!"

BY THE TIME MCGREGOR REACHED LEE'S BARN AT THE lower end of town there was a smear of watery-looking pink light along the easterly curve of the world. The chill that had been noticeable after midnight last night had increased until the gunsmith's fingers were stiffly uncooperative as McGregor dumped saddles and bridles in the runway, turned the animals into stalls, and walked on up through to Main Street. There was not a soul in sight. The town was tomblike as James stood a moment, looking toward the upper end of the road.

He knew which cubicle at the hotel was Fogarty's room, but he did not go up there. He went instead to his own building, fired up the little stove, put more water into the coffeepot. Then he went out back to scrub and to light up his little pipe as he sat quietly in thought for a while.

He was still sitting there when some zealous soul began ringing the church bell an hour before any sane person would be up and about.

The cafeman might not have fit into that category, although there were those among his customers who would have solemnly agreed that in fact he did sure as hell fit it; but at any rate his front window was fogged up by the time McGregor got down there to become the cafeman's first customer of the day.

Because they shared the distinction of not being great conversationalists, both the cafeman and the gunsmith did almost nothing to disturb the silent serenity of the morning until the cafeman brought McGregor's breakfast, filled his coffee cup, and said, "You seen Hugh? Mr. Dennis was lookin' for him last night."

James picked up his eating tools before answering. "Not since yestiddy."

The conversation ended there because McGregor filled his face with food and did not look at the cafeman, who shuffled back to his cooking area. He did very little business until after church, but because it paid to be prepared anyway, he got busy banging pots and pans around.

McGregor finished his meal about the same time daylight came swooping over the rooftops on the east side of Main Street to brighten Sheridan from one end to the other. That bell-ringer was still at it, and an occasional pedestrian appeared on the plankwalks, but when McGregor returned to the roadway chewing a toothpick, the jailhouse door still had its big brass lock in place.

He fretted until the unmistakable figure of Marshal Fogarty appeared across the road, hiking southward. McGregor spat out the toothpick and crossed over to wait until Fogarty arrived. They exchanged a terse greeting as Fogarty was unlocking the door. As he shoved it inward he said, "Get comfortable, James. I got to go over and get some breakfast for Jess Bell."

McGregor's clawlike hand shot out before Marshal Fogarty could move away. "Inside," the gunsmith snapped, and gave the larger man a rough shove. "Jess Bell can wait."

Fogarty's surprise blanked out what could have been a show of temper as he entered the office, turned, and stared at the smaller and older man.

McGregor spoke in clipped sentences from near the

184

doorway. When he had finished Marshal Fogarty went around behind the big old table that served as his desk, sat down, and looked unhappily at the gunsmith. He hadn't known McGregor had ridden out with Hugh last night, although if he'd been a little more wide awake he probably would have expected it; every other time one of them had headed into potential trouble the other one was with him.

"Broken leg, for crissake, out there near Barber's camp?"

McGregor nodded. "I'm no doctor, but it sure looked busted to me. But that's not what I'm down here about. He told me to tell you there's eight men at Barber's camp. An' that's not it either; what I want to know is how we're goin' to get Hugh away from there without Davy figurin' out that someone was sneakin' around his camp last night?"

Marshal Fogarty blew out a ragged, big breath and leaned back in his chair, staring at the ceiling. Eventually he spoke. "I got eleven possemen lined up to ride as soon as church lets out."

McGregor shook his head. "If you go out there all hell's goin' to bust loose. What's got to be done first is to get Hugh away from there."

"How, James? How do we go out there with a wagon and load him up and come back down here without Davy knowin' what we're doin' and figurin' out why we did it?"

Before the gunsmith could reply Marshal Fogarty sprang up and glared in the direction of his cellroom door. "How in the hell did he fall down that arroyo? Everything's ready here in town an' he had to break his leg."

McGregor's pale eyes smoldered. "Lots of folks bust

185

their legs. I never heard of anyone doin' it on purpose. It was dark last night, an' like I told you, that damned cow was out to gore someone. Joe, you sent him out there. If it wasn't for you he wouldn't be propped up in that thorn-pin thicket right now."

Hank Dennis appeared in the doorway wearing an elegant, go-to-meeting coat with a genuinely white shirt and a paisley scarf as a necktie. Even his boots had been shined. He nodded to Marshal Fogarty, but the man he really wanted to see, and whom the cafeman had said was over at the jailhouse, was sitting there looking more dour than usual.

Hank stepped inside as he addressed the gunsmith. "Where is Hugh?"

McGregor did not even look around as he replied. "Do I look like his mother?"

Dennis was taken aback. He looked inquiringly at big Joe Fogarty but got no help there, so he turned toward the gunsmith and spoke again. "James, I got to see him today while the preacher's still in town. It's about my girl's wedding. George wants Hugh to stand up with him, an' there's a practice weddin' to go through."

McGregor still did not look at the storekeeper, but he put a whimsical, ironic look upon the lawman as he said, "*Stand up* at a wedding?"

Fogarty jumped in very quickly to appease Hank Dennis. "We'll find him, Mr. Dennis. Maybe we won't be able to get him back here in time for the practice, but as soon as we can, we'll let you know."

After Dennis had left, scowling and mildly baffled by McGregor's attitude, James gazed at the bigger and younger man. "All right. You said we're goin' to get him down here. Now then, just how in hell do we do that?"

186

Fate had already taken care of that, but Joe Fogarty did not know it as he replied to the gunsmith. "Well . . . James, my plan is to go out there with the possemen, have them scatter into a big surround, and catch Davy's riders one at a time."

McGregor continued to regard the younger man. "Joe, if that works, fine. If it don't work Hugh's goin' to be sittin' out there suffering like the damned when the sun reaches into that thicket."

Fogarty threw up both arms. "You know a better way?"

"Yeah. Almost anything would be better. If you don't want to do it, I'll get a light wagon from Reg and go out there alone, an' if they stop me I'll tell 'em Hugh was headin' home from the mountains, didn't know they had a gather south of their camp, and a damned cow not only set him afoot but liked to have killed him, an' I'm out there to bring him back to town."

Fogarty scowled. "You think they'll believe that?"

"They'll have to believe it."

Fogarty shook his head. "You overlooked something, James. How would you know he was in that thicket unless you'd been out there with him? An' the minute you start your cock-and-bull story someone is goin' to think of that. Then what will you say? Nothing, because there won't be anything left but the truth. James, Davy's no fool. Sooner or later he's goin' to figure you'n Hugh was sneakin' around his camp last night, and he's goin' to wonder why, isn't he?"

McGregor sat dourly in his chair for a minute or two longer without speaking then pushed up to his feet and left the office without even looking back.

When he got up to his shop Hugh's apprentice was waiting. He looked worried. McGregor nodded brusquely at the younger man and went around behind his counter as he said, "I know. Hank Dennis came to the jailhouse when I was down there a little while ago. Son, all I can tell you is that Hugh'll be back as soon as he can."

George's gaze sharpened a little. "You know where he is?"

"Well . . . yes, but that's all I'm goin' to tell you, except that you'd ought to go back to the store and mind things until he can get back there."

George did not move. He watched McGregor puttering around, putting on his apron, checking the little stove and the coffeepot and the old battered saddlegun which was still clamped in his gun vise for the second day. Finally George turned toward the door, looking defeated as well as worried. McGregor relented as the youth reached the. doorway. "George, he'll be all right."

The big youth turned. "Is he hurt?"

"Well, not exactly. Not hurt enough so's he won't be all right directly."

"What happened to him? Where is he?"

McGregor had meant to be reassuring. He had not intended to get in any deeper than that, but the stubborn cast of the younger man's features and the sharp stare he was putting on the gunsmith made the older man inwardly writhe. McGregor was a direct individual. Deception was foreign to him. He fiddled with the knot on his apron while avoiding the younger man's stare.

The church bell began pealing again, louder and more insistent than before. McGregor looked toward the doorway and gently wagged his head. He had to raise his voice to be heard. "He got a little hurt last night. But like I told you, he'll be all right."

"When will he be back, Mr. McGregor?"

"Hell, I don't know, George, but I'm thinkin' on it. That's all I can tell you. When he gets back he can explain things to you—maybe."

There was no point in continuing this conversation. Even without the damned bell sending reverberations for a mile beyond town and making normal conversation impossible, everything had been said that James McGregor intended to be a part of.

George returned to the saddle-and-harness works, and James bent over the vise-gripped saddlegun. The bell continued to warn the faithful that services would commence on schedule, exactly at nine o'clock as they did every Sunday, and they had better shag their bones up there because, as everyone knew, once the reverend stepped into his pulpit the front doors were closed and would remain that way until the services were concluded.

Sheridan was inhabited by churchgoing folks, and like Hank Dennis, his wife, and daughter, people wore their best attire on Sunday. The actual number of genuinely devout Sheridanites would have been impossible to determine because it was the custom to attend services every Sunday morning. Not only in Sheridan, but all across the nation. It was a tradition, a custom, an ingrained human habit. As people everywhere did, the people of Sheridan trooped obediently to church every Sunday morning. Holdouts were few, and for financial reasons they were never local storekeepers; but every Sunday a few people fell asleep during the everlastingly repetitious sermons about sin, hell's fire, and damnation. Some simply sat with closed faces patiently waiting for things to end.

When the bell stopped ringing McGregor raised his

189

head a little waiting for it start again. When it didn't he knew the doors had been closed and that shortly now he'd be able to distantly hear most of the voices in town raised in song. He had nothing at all against religion; had over the years greased his boots, used his white shirt and clean trousers when he made an appearance, but he had no sense of guilt about failing to show up over there every blessed Sunday. As God certainly understood this particular Sunday, He would still be around next Sunday, but unless something was done to rescue old Hugh Pepperdine, *he* might not be.

People did not die from busted legs, unless of course they were also subjected to a boiling sun without a canteen, were as old as Hugh was, and just possibly might be found in their hiding place by men who wouldn't believe the most plausible lie an old harnessmaker could come up with.

After McGregor had considered and discarded a dozen ways to bring Pepperdine back in a wagon before this day was over, he had to settle on the one he and Marshal Fogarty had poked holes in down at the jailhouse: Simply get a rig from Reg Lee and drive out there in broad daylight, load Pepperdine in and start back, and when they were stopped by Davy's riders, lie, of course without too much expectation of being believed.

He shed his apron, rebuckled his gunbelt, put on an old hat, and went to stand with a cup of java in his hand while gazing out into the roadway for a moment before locking the shop and heading for the lower end of town.

Henry Pohl stopped out front, cupped both hands around his face, and peered through the window. When he saw James at the counter he walked in. "Where's Hugh?" he asked without any preliminaries.

190

McGregor eyed the doctor woodenly. "Not around, as far as I know."

"So I've found out. James? Why the gun and the hat? You goin' somewhere?"

"Henry, every time you walk past carryin' your little satchel do I ask you who is havin' a baby or got dog-bit or horse-kicked?"

Dr. Pohl could recognize a troubled human being when he saw one. "It's Hugh, isn't it?"

Instead of replying to the question James leaned down on the counter with his coffee cup and looked steadily at the younger man. "Supposin' a man busted his leg an' had to set out somewhere for about twenty-four hours; what would the results be?"

Henry Pohl stood in quiet thought for a while before speaking. "It would depend on a number of things, James. Is it a compound fracture? I mean, are there ends of broken bones showing through the flesh?"

"No. Just one hell of a swellin' with a sort of blue color."

"Where on the leg?"

"I think the ankle. That's where the swellin' is."

Dr. Pohl approached the counter, leaned on it looking straight at McGregor, and said, "Where is he?"

"Henry, I can't—"

"You'd better tell me, James. If it's a bad break, at his age the shock can kill a person. Where is he?"

". . . Out yonder in a thornpin thicket unable to stand up or walk."

Dr. Pohl did not ask how the injury had occurred; he said instead, "Why are you standing in here instead of going out to help him?"

"I am going. That's why I'm wearin' the gun and the hat. But it's close to Davy Barber's cow camp."

"When did he break it, James?"

"Last night. A damned fightin' cow charged us in the dark; Hugh didn't see the drop-off and rolled to the bottom of it."

"What were you doing out there in the dark?"

McGregor shifted his stance and looked broodingly past Henry's shoulder into the empty, roadway. "It's a complicated story," he murmured.

"Spying on Davy Barber, James?"

McGregor's eyes jumped back to the doctor's face. "Yes."

Dr. Pohl seemed poised to ask more questions. Instead he fished for a little notebook he was never without, touched a pencil to his tongue, and said, "Give me the exact directions to where Hugh is. Better yet, draw a map on that pad."

Horsemen passed by in the roadway, moving at a steady walk and riding in a closed-up group. They made very little noise. McGregor had finished drawing the map, and Henry Pohl was returning the little notebook to his pocket, when James looked up.

Davy Barber was in town with his riding crew! James did not even hear the voices raised in song up at the church. After the faded, weathered riders had passed he looked at Henry Pohl with widened eyes. "Hell, yes. Why didn't one of us figure that out before?"

Henry looked baffled. "Figure what out?"

"That he was waitin' for Sunday when everyone would be in church to bust his rangeboss out of the jailhouse."

Dr. Pohl twisted to look back, but the riders had passed; there was almost no dust to mark their passage, and James leaned to grab Henry's arm. "Go get Hugh," he said. "Never mind Barber. Him bein' in town'll make it easy for you to get Hugh into a wagon and fetch him back here."

CHAPTER 23

The Sunday Morning Massacre

AFTER THE DOCTOR'S DEPARTURE MCGREGOR EASED around his roadway door and looked southward. Davy and his riders hadn't tied up in front of the jailhouse; they had tied up over at the emporium that was directly opposite the jailhouse. McGregor did not dwell on this except to guess that Davy had done that on purpose.

He was standing with his armed riders, pulling off his gloves as he spoke. If Joe Fogarty was still in his office he should have seen them by now.

McGregor stepped back, sailed his old hat toward the counter, and inched forward again, yanking loose the tiedown thong that held his six-gun in its holster. Across the road there was a hint of movement in the shadows of Pepperdine's shop. James squinted until he saw Hugh's apprentice move into the doorway looking southward.

McGregor made a calculation: Counting himself, maybe the lad over yonder, and Joe Fogarty, there would be two men and a boy against eight rangemen.

They were singing again up at the church. This time the words came clearly. The hymn was "Rock of Ages." It had enough verses to keep the folks in there occupied for quite a spell. But it wouldn't make a hell of a lot of difference if they all emerged from the church anyway, because people did not wear guns in church.

McGregor was sweating as he watched Davy begin his march across to the jailhouse flanked by his riders. If

Joe was in there and resisted . . .

Hugh's apprentice called across the empty roadway. "What's he doing, Mr. McGregor? He's got the whole crew with him."

James did not reply.

Barber stepped up onto the plankwalk, turned, and looked both ways before turning toward the jailhouse again. He may have heard George, but if he had it didn't seem to bother him. McGregor counted them as they filed into Fogarty's office.

The silence was go deep, the hymn singing sounded close enough for James to pick out individual voices, but he didn't do that; he was watching the front of the jailhouse with total concentration.

George appeared in the harness shop doorway rolling up the apron he'd taken off. He was about to call over to McGregor again when the gunsmith held up his hand for silence. George stared at him, so James shook his head to emphasize the need for silence. George disappeared back into the shop, and McGregor forgot about him as he ran an idea through his mind: if he ducked into the back alley he could probably get down opposite the jailhouse. He had seven shotguns in a rack along the north wall.

It probably wasn't a good idea, but whether that was true or not he was distracted from considering it when George Jefferson appeared again in the harness shop doorway. He was wearing an old, holstered Colt on his right leg suspended from an equally old, half-filled shellbelt.

McGregor took a chance that the crowd inside the jailhouse office wouldn't hear him and spoke in only a slightly louder than normal voice.

"He's goin' to bust Jess Bell out of the jailhouse."

The big youth stared then leaned to peer southward. He did not say anything.

McGregor spoke again. "I think the marshal's in there."

The sound of a muffled gunshot cut across McGregor's last couple of words. He stiffened, waiting for more sounds of violence, but there were none and that, he thought, meant that the marshal had been shot.

He called to George again. "Wait until they come out with Bell."

Southward, among the buildings on the east side of Main Street, someone opened a door then slammed it closed. McGregor thought that had happened at the mercantile establishment, the cafe, or the bank. By a process of elimination he decided it had happened at the cafe, because neither the bank nor the emporium would have anyone in them on Sunday.

A flicker of movement snagged his attention across the road and southward, down where Henry Pohl's combination residence and clinic stood, but it was difficult to make out anything but mere movement at that distance. Because of the shadows cast across the porch by the overhanging roof, there appeared to be no more movement, or, if there was, McGregor could not make it out.

The singing had stopped. There was not a sound until a horse at the tie rack in front of the general store lustily blew its nose.

When McGregor looked toward the harness shop doorway again, it was empty. There was no sign of George.

If there'd been time for it, McGregor would have felt almighty lonely now that Hugh's apprentice had gone deeper into the shop. Or somewhere anyway, not out front where he would be needed.

A man in a gracefully curved, black hat stepped out to the middle of the plankwalk in front of the jailhouse. He had his right hand resting atop the saw-handle butt of a holstered gun as he turned methodically to study Main Street from south to north.

McGregor pressed back until he would be invisible, then turned swiftly, went to the wall rack, took down a shotgun, and stepped to a drawer to fumble with loads. He put six extra charges in a pocket, snapped the loaded gun closed, and returned to the doorway.

The black-hatted man had his back to the roadway, leaning with both hands on the doorjamb, looking into the jailhouse. He was talking, but McGregor couldn't even guess what he was saying except to imagine the man might be telling his companions the roadway was clear.

It was an elemental surmise since the rangemen had ridden into town for only one purpose. It was also an accurate one.

The man wearing the black hat turned, looked up and down Main Street one more time, jerked his head, and stepped off the plankwalk, his right hand again curled to draw the gun he wore.

McGregor's stare was riveted on the jailhouse doorway, but when they came out he couldn't be certain Jess Bell was among them, because as they left the building they did so all in a bunch.

The tension was as taut as a fiddle string as McGregor began to raise his shotgun. He finally saw the rangeboss, who was recognizable as his deliverers spread out slightly on their way across to where the man with the black hat was already freeing bridle reins. Bell's face was heavily bandaged. He was the only

196

hatless man among them, and although his injury was bad, he'd had plenty of time to recover from most of the pain; his unsteady gait as he was herded across the roadway puzzled McGregor.

They were among the saddle animals, moving efficiently and warily, when McGregor got the shotgun settled around the jamb of his doorway. At that distance he could pepper them but do little actual damage. He would wait until they turned up toward him and rode into range.

Without any warning a man's rough voice shouted into the stillness. "Hey, you sons of bitches!"

A single thunderous gunshot followed those words. The bullet tore splinters from a wooden post, and all hell broke loose. Barber's men were near enough to know where that challenge had come from. McGregor watched them jump clear of the animals to fire into the front of the cafe.

This was the precise moment when the advantage of surprise vanished. That gunfire sounded a mile beyond town in all directions, not to mention up as far as the church, where the doors were still closed.

McGregor stepped around the doorway, blew off one barrel, cocked methodically, and blew off the second barrel. The shattering explosions rattled windows on both sides of Main Street. Davy Barber's men squawked and fled for. shelter, even though McGregor's scattershot did them no damage. But it stung two of their horses. The animals flung backwards, snapped bridle reins, wheeled southward, and left town with their tails in the air like scorpions.

One of Barber's cowboys was somewhere near the brick bank building with a Winchester. He fired straight up the plankwalk toward the flash of McGregor's scattergun. It was good shooting; a sliver of doorjamb six inches long gouged the gunsmith's cheek, drawing blood. As McGregor instinctively jerked backward someone on the opposite side of Main Street yelled once and drilled the Winchester man straight through the brisket. Impact hurled him against a brick wall. He bounced off it as his hat fell aside, dropped his saddlegun, and fell forward, dead before he stopped moving.

They were confined to the area around the front of Dennis's store, the brick bank building, and the cafe. There was an empty lot between the store and the blacksmith's shop. One man ran like a deer. James was mopping his cheek, watching as the rider did not turn across the bare ground but raced for the protection of that big old freight wagon blocked up in front of the smithy.

He almost made it. In fact, he was slackening his pace a little, holding out one hand to grasp the protective side of the wagon, when a gunshot from somewhere in the vicinity of the jailhouse dropped him like a rock.

One man did make it around the side of the general store and out to the west-side alley across the empty lot, but no one knew that until later. Nor did anyone ever know who he was.

Two rangemen were forted up in the recessed doorway of the bank building, but with someone opposite them across the road somewhere who had killed two men without exposing himself, the pair of Barber-riders flung themselves out of their shelter and sped in different directions.

McGregor was reloading his shotgun, was snapping it closed, when he saw red muzzleblast from the doorway of the jailhouse and forgot to see whether either of the fleeing men had been hit because he was enormously relieved that Joe Fogarty was still alive. As he was hoisting the shotgun it crossed his mind that Fogarty had shot from very low, as though he had been on the floor of his office when he'd fired.

He had no time for additional speculation. One of those fleeing men was running wildly northward up the plankwalk, firing his six-gun in all directions as he ran.

McGregor stepped out into plain sight with the shotgun belt-buckle high. The oncoming man saw him, tried to check his momentum, couldn't do it, and threw up his gun. McGregor squeezed one trigger. As before, the sound was deafening. The cowboy was raised off the duckboards about a foot. His body started to fold forward from the top and bottom. McGregor's charge had nearly cut him in two.

As with any battle, no participant could see everything that happened, only the things they were immediately involved with McGregor was stepping back to the doorway when gunfire opposite the jailhouse swelled as though every man still standing was firing at the same time.

He caught a brief glimpse of a man whose face was turned away from him but whose attire and build were familiar, stepping straight forward with a six-gun in each hand as he fired.

The range was far too great for McGregor's remaining charge, nor did he think of making the attempt. He was awed by the rangeman's wildly savage defiance.

The man's legs were spread wide, his body was tilted slightly forward, his teeth were bared. That was the imprint McGregor would carry to the grave with him, and it only lasted a few seconds.

The returned gunfire broke one of the man's legs. He fell with the leg at an unnatural angle, propped himself on his good leg, and when the next flurry of slugs struck him, he still tried with all his ebbing strength to raise one gun.

There was a pause in the bedlam as the dying man used every ounce of strength he could still summon to aim one handgun in the direction of Henry Pohl's porch. Even as distant as McGregor was, when the dying man tugged the trigger the sound of a firing pin striking an empty casing was audible.

The man sank forward, put out a hand to ease the fall, and crumpled.

There was a moment of absolute hush. Even the echoes of the furious battle died as people burst out of the church at the other end of town yelling back and forth and running in every direction like frightened sheep.

McGregor turned back into his shop, got a piece of clean cloth, and held it to his bleeding cheek as he returned to the doorway with the shotgun in his free hand.

There were survivors down there, standing with their shoulders to the bank's brick wall, hands held high. One man kicked aside his shattered door and stepped outside with an ivory-handled six-gun cocked in his right hand as he padded toward the area of carnage.

McGregor shook his head. That damned disagreeable cafeman! He'd been the one whose profane outcry had started the fight. McGregor started down there. As he was approaching the front of the riddled cafe a tall, muscular man appeared from around behind the jailhouse climbing through pole stringers at the public corrals wearing a shirt plastered to him with sweat and dangling an old, long-barreled six-gun in one hand.

McGregor's stride faltered. So that's where Hugh's apprentice had gone; out the back of the shop into the alley and down where the battle started. James watched George move into the jailhouse doorway and wagged his head. Those two rangemen who had been shot dead at the beginning of the fight, one in front of the store, the second one trying to reach the protection of that old, blocked-up freight wagon, had been shot dead by someone over where George had come from.

McGregor halted near the sweating, unkempt cafeman. They exchanged a look. First McGregor smiled; second the disagreeable man in felt slippers smiled.

Suddenly there were townsmen still in their go-to-meeting clothes all over the place carrying shotguns, rifles, carbines, and handguns. There were no women or youngsters, but the fire-and-brimstone preacher was down there, without a weapon and with shocks of thick, curly hair hanging over his forehead as he went among the dead and injured.

Hank Dennis came up half out of breath to tug at James's sleeve. "Where's Henry? Joe Fogarty's been shot through the shoulder."

McGregor gazed dispassionately at the merchant then turned to cross the roadway through the bedlam in the direction of the jailhouse where three men, including George Jefferson, had hoisted big Joe Fogarty to a chair and were trying to make a blood-staunching bandage for the lawman's wound. McGregor leaned aside his shotgun but continued to hold the scarlet cloth to his face and tapped George on the shoulder.

When the youth turned McGregor smiled at him. "Hugh'll be proud of you."

"Is he back?"

"No, but he will be directly. Boy, I'm right proud of you, too."

CHAPTER 24

The Passage of Time

INCLUDING DAVY BARBER, WHOSE DEATH HAD BEEN the most spectacular, there were four dead rangemen. The injured included Joe Fogarty and a pair of Barber's riding crew. Of the three, Fogarty's loss of blood more than his wound put his survival in question, and since Henry Pohl did not return to town with Hugh in the wagon until just shy of suppertime, there was ample time for anxiety.

Only two rangemen had miraculously emerged from the battle unscathed. One of them was Jess Bell, the dazed individual whose delivery from Sheridan's jailhouse had prompted Davy Barber to lead his riders into a battle they should have been able to win if numbers had made that possible. He was roughly handled on his way back to a cell. The other rider was one of those young bull drivers who'd only arrived in the country a week or so earlier, and he was stunned speechless; simply stared at his red-faced interrogators and was ultimately thrown into another cell.

With nightfall imminent a harassed Dr. Pohl met McGregor in front of the harness shop. He examined the gouge that would scar McGregor for life, took him inside, cleaned the injury, and bandaged it. Then he was taken away by Rusty Morton and the old gaffer, who ran the abstract office, to hasten to his own residence to

202

care for Marshal Fogarty.

McGregor was still sitting on a stool in the harness shop when George appeared from out back, no longer armed, and spoke. McGregor was staring out into the roadway. George spoke again, then reached and shook the gunsmith until McGregor's head came around. George jerked a thumb. "Mr. Pepperdine wants to see you."

McGregor continued to sit for a moment, gazing at the boy who had reached manhood during a fifteen-minute period at the lower end of town.

"How is he?"

George reached and gently pulled McGregor off the stool. "Go see for yourself."

As James arose from the stool, he smiled. "You did yourself proud, son."

The younger man did not look proud. "He's waiting."

There was still considerable activity in the roadway. Almost every business establishment on both sides of the road was lighted. Men were calling back and forth, and shadowy silhouettes passed swiftly along on both sides of Main Street. Up at Morton's saloon there were plenty of customers but not very much conversation.

When McGregor stepped through the doorway of Hugh's lean-to quarters the gaunt old man on the bed, visible in yellowish lamplight, looked out from a tired, gray face and said, "One of 'em got away, eh?"

James didn't know that. He went to a chair, sat down, and said, "Gawddamndest mess you ever saw. I'll tell you somethin' that maybe I hadn't ought to. Davy went out like a Roman candle. I never saw anything like it. Countin' him there was four men killed, all rangemen."

"Anyone from town get hurt, James?"

McGregor went on speaking as though Hugh hadn't

opened his mouth. "I cut one in two across the road with a shotgun. George killed the other two. I couldn't swear to that, but he come from behind the jailhouse somewhere after it was over, and that's where the shots came from that killed them two." McGregor looked owlishly at his old friend whose bandaged foot and ankle looked as large as a flour sack atop the bedding. "How'd you make out?"

Hugh sighed. "George didn't say anythin' to me about killin' anyone."

"Well, most men don't talk about somethin' like that, do they?"

Hugh's gaze drifted from the gunsmith to his bandaged extremity. "You want to know something, James? Two little bones got broke but mostly it's a pulled tendon. Like a horse gets. But you know, I never in my misbegotten life had anythin' hurt as bad. . . . How's Joe?"

"I don't know. I saw them luggin' him over to the doctor's place but I haven't been over there yet. . . . Hugh, right at the time I felt fine."

Pepperdine smiled grimly. "Yes, I know. But right now you feel like someone's went and squeezed all the feelings out of you."

McGregor turned this over in his mind. He wasn't sure it was an accurate description, but he let it pass. "That damned fool liked to skunked us, Hugh. The reason he kept everyone in camp Saturday night was so's he could arrive down here early this mornin' when everyone was up yonder singing hymns."

Pepperdine barely nodded. He'd had plenty of time to reach the same conclusion. "You said he wasn't a fool."

McGregor shrugged. "Maybe he wasn't, but he sure as hell isn't around to prove it, is he?"

204

Pepperdine was already thinking of something else. "What's that feller's name who runs the cafe? Andy is all I ever heard him called."

"Andy Dexter. He saw 'em from inside the cafe, an' when they came out of the jailhouse he called 'em, an' that's when all hell busted loose. Hugh, I got to change my opinion of the cafeman."

"Uh-huh. Hank Dennis was in here a while back wringing his hands because I can't stand up."

"What'd you tell him?"

"That I wouldn't embarrass 'em at the wedding. I'd get a pair of crutches, but even if I had to crawl in there on my hands and knees, I'd be there."

McGregor gazed at his old friend. "Davy's dead. That leaves you'n me an' Joe Fogarty who know who the lad's father was."

"An' Henry. He figured it out."

"All right. An' Henry. The main thing is that the only person who might be spiteful enough to spill the beans is dead, an' the rest of us'll take the secret to the grave. But you know, I was settin' out front thinking about that. Four dead men, you'n Joe hurt, at least three, four other men's lives upset forever . . ."

Hugh gazed steadily at the gunsmith before speaking again. "If that's the price, then it's been paid and that's that."

McGregor roused himself from a relapse into another solemn reverie. "What'd Henry say about your leg? How long before you can put some weight on it."

"Maybe a month. Maybe longer. He said in older folks bones take forever to set, even little ones. An' the tendon—it could take a sight longer." Hugh made a harsh chuckle. "You know what he told me? That if I know what's good for me I won't get on a horse again

205

for six months. You know what I said to him? I'm not goin' to get on a horse for the rest of my life, an' I'm sure as hell not goin' to let Joe Fogarty dragoon me into any more of his damned troubles."

McGregor's expression showed a hint of a dry smile. "Partner, if you think back, this time it wasn't him dragooned anyone, it was you'n me got him involved in our effort to keep folks from knowin' about Davy's catch colt."

Pepperdine was adamant. "Well, whatever it was, I'm not goin' to step outside this shop except on business. I been lyin' here thinkin' that right now even old Silas up at the corralyard would look good to me."

McGregor finally laughed as he stood up. "You know damned well that's not goin' to be true once you're up and around. Hugh, I'm goin' to see Joe, but I'll be back. Anythin' you need?"

Pepperdine jutted his jaw toward an old trunk. "The lad turned me down. There's a bottle of malt whiskey in there. If you'd set it on this horseshoe keg beside the bed, I'd be beholden to you, James."

Later, when the gunsmith was passing through the shop and George looked inquiringly at him, he solemnly said, "He's resting. I'd leave him alone until morning if I was you."

Outside there was a noticeable coolness to the evening. Southward, a few men-shaped silhouettes were loitering where the fight had occurred, but one of the blessings of oncoming darkness was that little evidence was visible where men had died.

By the time McGregor reached Henry Pohl's place his mood had improved. Over at the cafe the window was steamed from the inside, which indicated that the cafeman had a counterful. McGregor hadn't eaten in many hours, but even with his improved feeling he still was not ready for food.

Henry's handsome wife admitted McGregor to the parlor where he remained until Henry, looking more harassed than ever, arrived. Henry nodded brusquely and led the way to the room where Joe Fogarty was lying inert as stone, with just his eyes showing signs of life.

McGregor looked at the doctor. Henry made a little frown and departed. Fogarty said, "Sit down," in a husky voice that sounded more exhausted than ill.

Most of his upper body was heavily bandaged. McGregor made a point of not looking at that as he said, "Hugh's comin' along."

Marshal Fogarty said nothing, but his eyes were fixed on the gunsmith.

James cleared his throat and looked around the severely plain little room before speaking again. "What happened at the jailhouse?"

"I was down in the cellroom with Jess Bell when they walked in. The first I knew who it was was when Davy called my name from up in the office doorway. He said for me to unlock Bell's door. I told him the keys was on a peg behind my desk in the office." Fogarty paused, reliving a moment he'd never forget. "The son of a bitch shot me. That's about all I remember until I come around with a battle goin' on out in the road. I crawled up there, the door was open, I could see them pinned to the stores over by the cafe. Everybody seemed to be firin' at the same time. I couldn't get up so I fired from the floor just inside the doorway."

McGregor nodded slowly. "You lost a lot of blood. You better just rest, Joe. I'll come back tomorrow."

But Marshal Fogarty's eyes were bright. "Did you see

Davy take us all on?"

"Yes."

"You ever see anything like that before, James?"

"No I never did, an' I'd just as soon not ever see anythin' like it again. Hugh's apprentice was either behind your jailhouse or south of it down near the corrals. He got two of those men sure as hell."

Fogarty sighed. "There's another mess."

"What?"

"Davy's dead. Four of his men are dead. They tell me one got away. Jess Bell an' another man are locked up."

"I know."

"Well, there are about three thousand Barber cattle out yonder eatin' up the countryside."

McGregor hadn't gotten around to thinking about that. He studied the design in some curtains surrounding a small window in the back wall. "I suppose we could scour up some fellers to mind them. Sure as hell Buster Henning would help."

"Yeah. Buster'll do it just to keep them off his grass. The question is, what do we do with them?"

McGregor returned his gaze to the man in the bed. He hadn't any idea, so he said, "Damned if I know."

"Find out if Davy had any next of kin, maybe down in Arizona. If he had, notify them. By the way, is that woman still in town we thought Davy was married to?"

McGregor had no idea about that either. "Why?"

"Because Henry took Davy's wallet off the corpse. There was eight hundred dollars in it. I'd like to see that she gets it."

McGregor stared at Fogarty. "Can you give it to her legal?"

Joe didn't bat an eye. "No."

They exchanged stares for a moment, then McGregor

208

inclined his head. "Is it cash greenbacks?"

"Yes."

"Well, I sure never saw it an' don't know anything about it. You're most likely in a delirium anyway. How's the shoulder comin' along?"

"Henry's an old mother hen. I'll be up an' around in a few days."

McGregor was arising when he spoke next. "You better do what Henry says. What I saw of you after the fight, you looked like a big wad of freshly butchered meat."

Henry appeared to hasten the gunsmith's departure. Out on the porch they conversed briefly about Fogarty's recovery, and as McGregor walked away he decided Joe was probably pretty accurate; Henry was an old mother hen. Except for looking a little peaked, it seemed to McGregor the marshal's vital juices were about as strong as ever.

The event that helped Sheridan recover was the wedding of George Jefferson and Charlotte Dennis. McGregor spent half the morning brushing the only pair of pants he owned that had a coat to match them. He had to give up on the damn hat. He could brush away the accumulation of dust, but there was nothing he could do to hide the sweat stains.

When he was ready to lock up and join the promenade of local folks in the direction of the church, Hugh Pepperdine appeared across the road, teetering on a pair of handmade crutches. He was wearing a spanking new dark hat on the back of his head with unruly, iron-gray hair sticking out on all sides. He called a rough greeting across the road, and said, "How d'you like this suit?"

McGregor admired it. "Is Hank havin' a sale?"

"No," responded the harnessmaker, crutching his way in McGregor's direction. "He said he couldn't charge any more'n he gave for it, seein' as how him an' me'll be sort of related directly. I gave him four dollars for it. Let's get along or there won't be any chairs left and standin' with these things in your armpits don't make a man feel a lot like smiling."

The roadway was clogged with wagons, buggies, some light ranch rigs and scores of saddle animals, and inevitably some damned fool had arrived on a stallion. He'd tethered his animal to a stud ring embedded in a huge old cottonwood well away from the other horses, but throughout the ceremony that agitated horse with mare-scent all around would occasionally let go with a stud-horse bawl.

The first couple of times it was ignored, then someone near the rear of the crowded church closed the roadway doors. That deadened the sound but did not entirely mitigate it. Old Silas Browning, perched on a bench behind McGregor and Pepperdine, for once without his big hat, leaned to make a chortling whisper. "Real appropriate, wouldn't you gents agree? One out there tied to a tree snortin' up mares an' another one in here standin' up there in front of the preacher."

Hugh reddened. Neither he nor the gunsmith acted as though they had heard, but shortly after the ceremony was completed and they were filing out of the church with Silas stumping along in front of them, they exchanged a wintery look.

Outside the solemnity vanished. People threw rice and at least one ingenious soul had tied a string of odds and ends to the rear of the top buggy George and Charlotte climbed into for the drive to the Dennis house for the reception.

Not everyone went to the reception. Neither Hugh nor James did; neither did old Silas, who went scuttling toward his corralyard, making his annoying sniffing sound because he'd been obliged to waste the whole blessed morning. Weddings were mandatory, receptions were not.

When Pepperdine and McGregor entered the harness works, emptiness jumped out at Hugh. For the first time in almost a year he'd walked into his shop when there wasn't even a scrap of leather on George's worktable.

McGregor waited patiently for his friend to set up the below-the-counter bottle. It did not occur to him until he'd had two jolts that Hugh was talking more and louder than he normally did. James turned that over in his mind while considering the swept-clean worktable, then removed his string tie and deliberately dropped it into the gaboon. He'd hated neckties all his life. As he looked up Hugh was hoisting his hip pockets onto a stool so he would be free of the damned crutches. He smiled at McGregor.

"I'm goin' to miss the lad, James."

McGregor nodded, his dour personality back in place. "That son of a bitch Barber marked us all. Some worse'n others. Davy had eight hunnert dollars in his wallet."

Hugh's eyes widened at the amount. It was about what he made all year long. "That's a lot of money to be carryin' around."

McGregor had no comment to make about that. He was regarding the bottle, not his old friend, when he said the rest of it. "Joe's goin' to give it to that lady we thought Davy was married to."

Pepperdine's reaction to that was simply to nod his head in agreement with the notion. After a moment he

211

asked a question. "What about the cattle and all out at Davy's cow camp?"

"Joe's goin' to see if Davy had any heirs."

Hugh gazed at the backs of his scarred, work-roughened hands. "Seems his catch colt should get some of the estate, don't it?"

McGregor flared up. "You know a damned sight better'n that."

Hugh had to agree. "I guess so."

On that note they parted. They did not meet again for several days, not until they saw with surprise that Joe Fogarty was slowly but resolutely making his way in the direction of the jailhouse. Eleanor Pohl had fed him up and babied him like a butcher steer. Later, along toward evening, they saw him walking up in the direction of the roominghouse, but he did not go up that far; he turned in at Henry Pohl's residence, met Eleanor at the door, and she told him her husband was out back at the embalming shed. All he said to Eleanor was that he couldn't find Harriet Blake up at the hotel.

Henry was embalming an old man from among the shacks at the lower end of town when Joe walked in and went right on working until Joe had told him about Harriet Blake; then he picked up an old towel to dry his hands on, pulled a length of canvas over the cadaver, and spoke in a detached manner. "When folks die they take secrets to the grave with 'em. When they leave the country they do the same thing. The real story is buried with Missus Jefferson."

Fogarty nodded. "I reckon. Maybe my prisoners will talk before the circuit rider comes to town to set up court. But that woman—"

"That woman," the doctor said, interrupting Fogarty while still gazing at the shrouded corpse on his worktable, "told my wife she wanted to go down to Buttonwillow to be with her daughter."

Fogarty asked a question. "Did she leave an address down there with Eleanor?"

"No. Why?"

"Just wondered. She won't be hard to find."

Henry tossed the old towel aside and raised his eyes to the marshal's face. "I prepared those rangemen for burial."

"Yeah. I know. If you want to put in a claim against Davy's estate—"

"Let me finish, Joe. Those men were killed by forty-five slugs." Henry paused, still looking straight at the town marshal. "Davy was hit five times. One leg was broken, and he was hit alongside the ribs and through the left arm. None of those slugs would have killed him."

Fogarty got a vertical crease between his eyes. "Then what the hell did kill him?"

Henry fished in a pocket and removed something that shone dully from a coppery-colored coating. He held it in his palm for the marshal to inspect. "This is what killed him. It's from some kind of a little handgun; maybe about a thirty-two caliber. It nicked his aorta. He was bleeding to death internally when he went down for the last time on his face."

Fogarty examined the small pellet. It was nearly intact except for a slight abrasion on one side where it had struck bone. Joe scowled at the doctor. "Who had a gun like that?"

"You want to see it? Come along, it's in the parlor."

"Wait a minute. Who owned it, Henry? Do you know who fired it?"

"Yes. The person who fired it went out to my front

213

porch when the fight started. It was Harriet Blake. When the fight started, Eleanor saw her grab the gun from behind a picture in our parlor and rush out to the porch. Eleanor saw her aim the gun with both hands and fire point-blank as Davy was shooting in all directions with a weapon in each hand. When Davy went down the woman returned to the parlor, put the gun back behind the picture of my parents on the sideboard, and left the house. She went up to the hotel."

Joe considered the little bullet again, briefly this time, before dropping it into a shirt pocket as he gazed at Henry Pohl. "Now what?" he muttered.

The doctor said, "It's up to you. She deliberately killed him as surely as you and I are standing here right this minute. She came to town with that gun in her purse, and if I had a thousand dollars I'd bet every cent of it she came here to kill Davy with it."

Joe said, "Everyone was shootin' out there."

Dr. Pohl nodded. "Yes. So it was self-defense wasn't it? The cause of Davy's death was a gunshot wound in the chest during a fight. Eleanor will testify to that if she has to. Joe, we both know what was the cause of Davy's death. We also know the *reason*, don't we?"

When Marshal Fogarty continued to stand there in scowling silence the doctor added one more thing to what he'd already said. "Get something settled in your mind, Joe."

"Get what settled, for crissake?"

"That in this instance there wasn't any connection between justice and the law, and if you or anyone else tries to prove otherwise, they'll never be able to do it."

Fogarty's scowl deepened. "You don't have to preach to me. I'm satisfied she was justified. Even if I didn't know her real reason for killin' Davy, I'd still say she

214

was justified—the damned fool was shootin' at everyting in sight. Henry, I got to get back to my office."

But Marshal Fogarty didn't go back there. He went up to his quarters at the roominghouse. Aside from the interlude in the embalming shed, he'd been overdoing it a little lately.

It was four days later, when he was sitting in his office with Buster Henning, that Hugh and James walked in. Buster nodded at the older men but said nothing. He and the marshal had been discussing the completed roundup of Davy's cattle. Buster was worried about no one being out there full time to keep the animals from drifting, and Joe Fogarty was worried about the fact that, although he'd sent a letter to Davy's nearest town down in Arizona ten days earlier (the same day he mailed eight hundred dollars to Harriet Blake down in Buttonwillow), he'd received no reply.

As Hugh leaned his crutches aside and sat down he tossed a limp yellow envelope atop Fogarty's desk. "Telegram," he said. Before Joe could ask the obvious question Hugh gave him the answer. "Silas brought it to my shop where James an' I was havin' coffee. True to type he wouldn't walk all the way down here to deliver the thing. It was addressed to you through the telegraph office down in Bordenton. Jack Carpenter was ready to leave down there on his Sheridan run when the telegrapher ran over and told him to bring it up here."

Fogarty opened the envelope, and with three sets of eyes on him, spread the folded paper flat; then he smiled widely as he handed the paper to Buster Henning. "There's your answer about Davy's cattle. I didn't know he had a brother. He'll get up here next week with some riders to take the cattle south with him. If he's a better man than Davy was—and hell, almost anyone is—he'll be willin' to pay you for rounding them up."

Henning arose, looking more relieved than pleased. After his departure the pair of older men continued to sit there in silence until Joe addressed them. "I sent the money to that woman down in Buttonwillow. And one of these evenings, when all we got to do is sit in the saloon to keep cool, I'll tell you a story about how Davy died you might have a little trouble believing."

They continued to sit there, saying nothing, until Hugh finally reached for his crutches, got them positioned, and hoisted himself upright. As he was swinging toward the roadside door he smiled at Joe Fogarty. "It was the damndest mess I ever been through. It only started out as a way to keep anyone, includin' my apprentice, from knowin' he was Davy Barber's catch colt."

Fogarty leaned on his table looking at the older men. He faintly smiled. "Next time don't you two drag me into one of your messes."

McGregor reddened. "Our messes, you oversized coot; you're the law around here, we aren't."

After they had left his office Fogarty leaned back and laughed.

We hope that you enjoyed reading this
Sagebrush Large Print Western.
If you would like to read more Sagebrush titles,
ask your librarian or contact the Publishers:

United States and Canada

Thomas T. Beeler, *Publisher*
Post Office Box 659
Hampton Falls, New Hampshire 03844-0659
(800) 818-7574

United Kingdom, Eire, and
the Republic of South Africa

Isis Publishing Ltd
7 Centremead
Osney Mead
Oxford OX2 0ES England
(01865) 250333

Australia and New Zealand

Bolinda Publishing Pty Ltd
17 Mohr Street
Tullamarine, Victoria, 3043, Australia
1 800 335 364